His eyes pierced hers. "You really don't have any idea what you do to a man, do you? I'm going to kiss you so you'll find out."

Guido's intensity shook her, and then his head descended and his mouth closed over hers. Enveloped in heat, she felt his hands roam over her back and hips, urging her closer so she could feel every hard muscle and sinew in his body.

Though Dea had been with a few men who'd wanted to kiss her passionately, she hadn't fully reciprocated. Something had always held her back…until now.

This was different. Guido was different.

The feel of his mouth slowly devouring hers created such divine sensations she felt she'd been born for this moment and couldn't get enough.

"Guido…" she gasped in pleasure as he drew her into wine-dark rapture.

She clung to him. They were moving and breathing like they were a part of each other. Emotions greater than she could describe had taken over now that Guido had swept her into his arms.

Dear Reader,

I thought a lot about my Italian hero for this, my latest book, *The Billionaire's Prize*. Because of his exceptional looks and gifts he's been in the public eye and sought-after by women since his teens. The man hasn't ever known real rejection until he meets my heroine.

When I did a little research for this novel I found an article about the kinds of rejection a man can meet in life. Four were listed: evil and cold-blooded rejection, lukewarm rejection, not-that-into-you rejection and self-imposed rejection.

None of those four exactly covered what happens to my hero, but the author of the article made the following comment, which he came up with while surfing. He said that a person can suffer physical pain when held down under a big wave. It can be frightening. And that got him thinking that physical pain cannot usually be controlled. So what's worse? Physical or emotional pain?

He went on to say, 'When you go for a girl and get rejected it's emotional, and emotional pain is *totally under your control*. It's all in how you frame it and deal with it. Everyone faces rejection and failure in life—that's just part of the game. If you're not taking big risks, you're not going to score those big waves and those gorgeous women!'

That's true. So I'm going to leave it to you, my dear reader, to read the book and figure out how best to describe my hero's pain, and how he finally deals with it to achieve his heart's desire.

Enjoy!

Rebecca Winters

THE BILLIONAIRE'S PRIZE

BY
REBECCA WINTERS

Published in Great Britain 2016
By Mills & Boon, an imprint of HarperCollins*Publishers*
1 London Bridge Street, London, SE1 9GF

ISBN: 978-0-263-06569-5

Our policy is to use papers that are natural, renewable and recyclable
products and made from wood grown in sustainable forests. The logging
and manufacturing processes conform to the legal environmental
regulations of the country of origin.

Printed and bound in Great Britain
by CPI Antony Rowe, Chippenham, Wiltshire

Rebecca Winters lives in Salt Lake City, Utah. With canyons and high alpine meadows full of wildflowers, she never runs out of places to explore. They, plus her favourite vacation spots in Europe, often end up as backgrounds for her romance novels—because writing is her passion, along with her family and church. Rebecca loves to hear from readers. If you wish to email her, please visit her website at cleanromances.com.

Books by Rebecca Winters

Mills & Boon Romance

The Vineyards of Calanetti
His Princess of Convenience

The Montanari Marriages
The Billionaire's Baby Swap
The Billionaire Who Saw Her Beauty

Greek Billionaires
The Millionaire's True Worth
A Wedding for the Greek Tycoon

The Greek's Tiny Miracle
At the Chateau for Christmas
Taming the French Tycoon
The Renegade Billionaire

Visit the Author Profile page at millsandboon.co.uk for more titles.

PROLOGUE

DEA CARACCIOLO STOOD inside the grand dining hall of the castle on Posso Island. She was ready to flee now that she'd done her part during the wedding ceremony of her twin sister, Alessandra, and Rinieri Montanari.

"Darling? Why are you here by the doors?"

Oh, no. She turned her head in surprise. "Mamma."

"I still need to be in line to greet the guests and would like you to go sit with Guido and his parents."

Dea didn't think she could bear it. "Please don't make me."

"But you're the maid of honor. Your father and I are depending on you to entertain the best man and his family. Alessandra says they love Rini, and Signor Rossano has spoken highly of you since the night you were a model in the fashion show on his yacht. Come on. I'll walk you over to their table."

The mention of the yacht increased her agony, but this was one situation Dea couldn't get out of. Somehow she would have to endure Guido's company for a few more minutes.

During the wedding ceremony they'd gone through

the motions to be civil to each other in order to carry out their duties, but he'd hardly looked at her and she knew why. He couldn't help but have a low opinion of her since that night on the yacht when she'd made the worst blunder of her life with Rini in front of Guido. He probably assumed she was still in love with her new brother-in-law.

The situation couldn't be uglier, but her mother expected her to be gracious for a little while longer. When they approached the table, Guido and his father got to their feet before inviting her to sit down.

Guido's mother was a lovely woman and Dea tried to concentrate on her once they started to eat. "My sister told me about your generous gift to her and Rini."

"We thought they should honeymoon on our yacht to get away from everyone else. Alessandra is perfectly charming, and Rini's a favorite of ours."

"So I've heard."

"I have to say, you looked so beautiful the night of the fashion show," Signora Rossano continued. "But tonight you're even more beautiful."

"Thank you," she whispered.

"It's only the truth," a smiling Signor Rossano interjected. "Don't you think so, Guido?"

His son put down his champagne glass. "Papà? As you well know, Signorina Caracciolo has most of the Italian male population at her feet."

His father nodded with satisfaction. "That is true."

To his parents' ears, Guido's comment must have sounded like a supreme compliment. But the choice of the word *most* let Dea know he didn't include himself in that particular population.

"Signor Rossano, the other models and I were amazed you would allow your yacht to be used for a fashion show backdrop. It was a great thrill for them and they're hoping you'll offer it again."

"I wouldn't count on it for another year," Guido murmured out of his father's hearing, sounding turned off by her comment. She hadn't meant that she included herself in those who hoped to wangle another invitation. But no doubt Guido had assumed as much. She shouldn't have said anything at all.

Feeling more and more uncomfortable, she almost gasped with relief when her aunt Fulvia came over to the table and asked her if she'd like to say goodbye to the Archbishop of Taranto, who'd married her sister and Rini. It was a great honor and Dea excused herself with as much grace as she could muster before clinging to her aunt's arm. Her mother's only sister had saved her from further embarrassment and she would always be grateful.

CHAPTER ONE

One year later

"SIGNORA PARMA IS expecting you. Walk back through the doors to her workshop."

Dea Caracciolo thanked the receptionist and headed for the inner sanctum of the world-renowned Italian opera-costume designer. The only reason Dea had been given this privilege was because her aunt Fulvia and Juliana Parma were such close friends.

Though Dea had met Juliana and her husband on many occasions at her aunt's southern Italian *castello* in Taranto, this particular meeting wasn't social and the outcome—good or bad—would rest entirely on Dea's shoulders.

The sought-after redheaded designer in her late sixties stood surrounded by her staff, giving orders to one and all in her flamboyant style. When she saw Dea, she motioned her to come closer and clapped her hands.

"Everyone?" Their eyes fastened on Dea. "You've all known Dea Loti as Italy's leading fashion model.

She's actually Princess Dea of the Houses of Carac-ciolo and Taranto and the niece of my dear friend Princess Fulvia Taranto. But while she's here working with me during her spring-semester designer course at the Accademia Roma, you will call her Dea and accord her every courtesy."

Dea was so surprised she blurted, "You mean you're willing to take me on without talking to me about it first?"

"Of course. Fulvia has told me everything I need to know, so I called the head of your department and asked them to send you to me."

Dear Fulvia. Dea loved her so much. "I can hardly believe this is happening."

"Believe it! You're even more beautiful than the last time we were together. Imagine if you were a so-prano in the opera too—you would have every tenor in the world dying of love for you."

Heat filled Dea's cheeks. "How awful." Once upon a time Dea would have liked to hear a compliment like that, but not since she'd been in therapy to help her get on the road to real happiness.

Juliana chuckled. "Come in my private office."

The others smiled as she followed the older woman into a small cluttered room that still managed to be tidy. Dea handed her a small bouquet of roses.

"What's this?"

"A token of my gratitude that you even agreed to meet with me."

"*Grazie*, Dea." She inhaled the perfume from the

flowers. "Heavenly. Fulvia must have told you how much I love pink roses."

"I remember your husband giving you some after the opera a year ago."

"You're a very sweet and observant young woman. You're going to go far in this business. I feel it in my bones."

Sweet? That wasn't a word one would apply to the Dea of the past. The old Dea was too self-absorbed. She'd learned a lot about herself in therapy. The new Dea was working on thinking about others.

Juliana put the flowers in a bowl and sank into the chair behind her desk. "Sit down, my dear." Dea did her bidding. "What's this news that you've given up modeling?"

"It's true. I did one show at the end of last semester, but my goal is to become a period costume designer for the opera, like you. As you know, I've loved costume design from the time I was a child. You have no idea how excited I am to work with an expert like you and learn all I can. It's a great privilege."

Juliana's brown eyes sparkled. "You're going to love the project I'm winding up now. It's the costuming for *Don Giovanni*, which will go into production the third week of May. I'd like to hear your comments on this new sketch for Donna Elvira." She thrust a rendering into Dea's hands.

Don Giovanni was one of Dea's favorite operas. But the second she saw the drawing, she shot Juliana a glance. "Don't you mean Donna Anna?"

A smile broke the corner of Juliana's mouth. "Bravo,

Dea. Nothing gets past you. This costume is indeed meant for a younger woman. I've always known you to have a discerning eye. In fact I remember the fashion shows you used to put on at the *castello* with your sister when you were little. They were delightful and, in some instances, brilliant!"

Brilliance was a quality one attributed to Alessandra, not Dea. The unexpected compliment sent a curl of warmth through her body. Juliana handed her another drawing from a pile on her desk. "*Here* is a first draft of the costume for Donna Elvira that she'll wear in the dark courtyard scene. One of the staff worked it up."

Dea studied it for a few minutes. Her brows formed a frown.

Juliana chuckled. "Don't be afraid to tell me exactly what you think. I've always admired your honesty."

Coming from Juliana, that kind of praise meant a great deal.

"In my mind this gown is too frivolous and doesn't reveal her true character. I see Donna Elvira as a mature woman who's ahead of her time. She's hurt and outraged with Don Giovanni for his abandoning her. I'd like to see her gown toned down to convey that she's anything but a fool. She's been on a mission to find him."

"I agree completely. Bring me your version by tomorrow at 11:00 a.m." She took back the drawing and rose to her feet. "That's all the time I can give you for now."

"Mille ringraziamenti, signora."

"Juliana, *per favore.*"

Dea rushed around the desk to give her a kiss on the cheek. "I'm more grateful than you know for this opportunity."

After saying those words, she left the building and took a taxi back to her apartment. Located in the heart of Rome, the elegant complex she lived in was in walking distance of the Pantheon and the Piazza Navona. It had been home to her for quite a while. She loved the ancient street, which was over five hundred years old, with its dozens of wonderful shops. On this particular Monday, the lovely April weather matched her lightened mood.

Once she'd eaten lunch she would get to work designing a gown already forming in her mind. But first she needed to make an important phone call to her aunt, who'd made this unexpected meeting with Juliana possible.

When the older woman answered, Dea said, "Zia Fulvia?"

"Dea, how wonderful to hear from you! Your mother is here with me. I'll put the phone on speaker so we can both talk to you."

"Mamma?"

"Darling. I've been anxious to hear from you."

Her heart pounded with excitement. "Guess what? Juliana called my department at the Accademia and has taken me on. I've been given my first assignment. And it's all thanks to you, Fulvia."

"Juliana wouldn't have offered to help you if she

didn't already think you could do the job. When you break out on your own one day, your résumé will be worth its weight in gold because you'll have worked under her tutelage."

"I know that and I'm so thrilled! It's all because of you that I'm finally going to fulfill my dream! Now I've got to prove myself."

"I have no doubt of it."

"Neither do I," her mother said. "I don't think I've heard you this happy in years!"

Tears stung Dea's eyes. "This is the beginning of my new life."

"Your father's going to be overjoyed with this news."

"You've both given me wonderful advice and told me my future is out there waiting for me. Being able to work with Juliana, I know I'm going to find it!"

"Good for you, darling."

"I love you and will call you later."

She hung up, eager to get started on a design that would convince Juliana she hadn't been wrong to do this enormous, unprecedented favor for Fulvia. Dea had meant it when she'd said this was the beginning of her new life.

While she'd been in therapy this last year, she'd been forced to dig deep into her psyche to understand what made her tick. She'd been given several assignments to work on: forget self, put other people first and be kind before blurting out something she'd regret, even if it was true.

But her assignment to let go of the pain of the past was easier said than done. She had to stop dwelling on the fact that her identical twin sister, Alessandra, had been the one to attract the gorgeous engineering magnate Rinieri Montanari, not Dea, in an incident that had brought on Dea's emotional crisis.

She'd met Rini and his best friend Guido Rossano on board the fabulous Rossano yacht during a modeling assignment in Naples. Though Dea had been the first to meet Rini and had fallen for him on the spot—even kissing him passionately in front of Guido before saying good-night—Rini hadn't been interested in her.

When she looked back on that now, she was mortified to imagine what Guido must have thought of her behavior. As for Rini, she'd never expected to see him again. But to her shock, he met Alessandra while he was on business in the south of Italy. That was all it took for the elusive bachelor to fall in love and marry her sister.

Dea had been crushed and her serious loss of confidence had required professional help. Through therapy it became clear that, among other things, she'd always been jealous of her sister's intelligence and scholastic success. Alessandra had already written and published an important factual historical book on their ancestor Queen Joanna.

But it was her aunt Fulvia's comment that had brought her up short and made her realize she needed help.

Dea Caracciolo, do you want to conquer every man you meet? What would you do with all of them? It's not natural.

Her aunt had been right. It wasn't natural. Despite Dea's attempt to flirt with Rinieri, he hadn't been drawn to her. Period.

Following her conversation with Fulvia and her mother, Dea had gotten counseling and had been going through a difficult, painful period of self-evaluation and remembered mistakes. Her darkest memory had involved Alessandra's first love years earlier.

He'd pursued Dea. Part of her had felt guilty, yet another part had been flattered when he'd followed her back to Rome, where she was modeling at the time. But he'd turned out to be a man incapable of being faithful to any woman. A torturous time had followed for her and Alessandra. Only in the last year had they finally put the pain of that experience behind them and had become close in a new, honest way.

Still, trying to find one's self was not an easy journey. Though being a top fashion model had initially brought her excitement and a lot of interest from men, in time Dea hadn't found the fulfillment she craved in a career she'd always known couldn't last forever.

As was brought out in therapy, those deep longings for inner contentment had eluded her. She knew she would have to change her focus if she was going to have a happy life like her parents, or like Alessandra, who was now ecstatically married and a new mother. Because of a soccer injury, Rini hadn't been able to give her children, so they'd adopted little Brazzo. Dea couldn't be happier for them.

After serious thought, she'd chosen to follow her

natural inclination and make her way in a new direction that used her brain and God-given talents rather than her looks, but she was still filled with anxiety.

Forget self.

That's what her brilliant underwater-archaeologist sister had done. In the process, she'd won a wonderful man and already had a family.

Somewhere out there, Dea's prince existed. As her wise mother had promised her, "One day he'll find *you*. In the meantime, work on finding yourself, darling."

Friday afternoon Guido paused at the door of the soccer store adjoining his suite of offices in the Stadio Emanuele soccer stadium in Rome. "I'm leaving now, Sergio. As usual I'll be back Sunday morning before the big game. Have a good weekend."

"You too, boss." His administrative assistant smiled because he thought he knew why, when he could, Guido spent every Friday night and Saturday away from Rome, unable to be reached by anyone. But Sergio would be dead wrong about the reason.

Guido eyed his spectacular soccer mate from the past, whose serious leg injury at the height of his game prevented him from ever competing again. Now that Guido was the owner of a minor national soccer team, he'd recruited Sergio to do a little of everything.

The man knew more about the ins and outs of the national soccer league than anyone. He not only ran their business and ticket sales with meticulous care, but he kept the museum and their soccer store stocked and profitable. On top of that, he handled the phones and kept out unexpected visitors unless they made appointments.

"How come you haven't left already, Sergio? You work too hard. As far as I know you haven't taken a break in months." The man screened Guido's incoming phone calls from the media, but most important, those from Guido's hovering parents.

Being an only child, Guido realized they'd had a hard time accepting that he'd taken a year off from the Leonides Rossano Shipping Company to pursue an old soccer dream. Guido loved them and stayed in touch, but he'd felt smothered and enjoyed the freedom his new career was giving him away from the family business.

"Work saves me from my demons," Sergio commented. Guido could relate to that. "Don't you know there are tons of women calling here all the time after hours, or wanting to order stuff online? You're still a poster hero with those who remember you winning those past championships."

"Even after ten years?" Guido smiled wearily. "I leave all the fans to you. As I see it, you've been divorced long enough and need to find someone who can accept your passion for the sport. You had a big female following of your own."

He scoffed. "That all ended after my marriage. I don't think there is such a woman."

Neither did Guido, but he kept that comment to himself. "Try to enjoy yourself this weekend."

"I know *you* will," Sergio fired back. "Go ahead

and keep it to yourself, but you can't tell me you don't have a woman somewhere."

Conversation over. "Ciao, Sergio," he called to his friend before shutting the door.

There'd never been a lack of women for Guido. In his late teens he'd gotten into a serious relationship with one of the most popular girls at school, Carla, but over time he discovered she loved his celebrity status, not him. From that point on, he was wary of women.

The shock of learning she didn't truly love him changed his perspective on the dating experience. After that, Guido continued to enjoy women, but he didn't get into any more serious relationships. His soccer life had been so full, he'd put the idea of settling down out of his mind.

However, there'd been one woman over the last year who'd taken his breath and was still unforgettable. Dea Loti. Italy's most famous model. Her lesser-known name was Dea Caracciolo.

He'd met her aboard his father's yacht during a fashion show taped for television. It had been galling to realize she'd looked right through him in order to pursue his lifelong friend Rinieri Montanari, and it had aroused Guido's jealousy.

That emotion was something that had never happened to Guido before. He'd tried to put it away because Rini was the best, but it still haunted him.

Guido left the stadium in his Lamborghini and headed straight for the airport. By dinnertime his private jet, with the logo of Scatto Roma—the name of his soccer team, which meant *surge* in Italian—

landed at a private runway just outside Metaponto in Southern Italy. Rini would be waiting on the tarmac for him in the Jeep. They had a lot to catch up on.

Through a quirk of fate, his best friend had married Alessandra Caracciolo, Dea's identical twin sister. Since the wedding, the couple had been spending part of the time at Rini's villa in Positano and the rest of it at her family's island *castello*.

Montanari Engineering, located in Naples, was now drilling for oil on Caracciolo land in Southern Italy, thus the reason for meeting Rini here on the island.

After learning his friend had become a father, Guido had invited Rini for a meal at his apartment in Rome. But this would be the first time Guido had been back to the island since Rini's wedding to Alessandra when he'd been best man. They'd issued him many invitations to come, but Guido had turned them down, using business as the excuse. In reality, he didn't want to take the chance of seeing Dea again.

By now it shouldn't bother him that the woman who'd been so fascinated by Rini while they were on the Rossano yacht was none other than Alessandra's sister. Dea had been her maid of honor. After the wedding ceremony, she'd sat down to dinner with Guido and his parents. While she talked to them, all he could see was her kissing Rini before saying good-night to him on board the yacht.

But that was a year ago. Time had passed and he knew her modeling career took her all over Italy. He was certain she wouldn't be here at the castle. If Rini had mentioned otherwise, Guido wouldn't have accepted the invitation.

As he exited the plane he could see Rini.

"Your team name is perfect," his friend called out the window of the Jeep on the tarmac. "You *are* surging. Bravo."

"Grazie."

When Guido climbed in the Jeep, his first sight of his dark-haired friend said it all. "Fatherhood agrees with you. How is *piccolo* Brazzo?"

"He's going to be a soccer player for sure."

"I can't wait to see him."

"I'm sorry. Not this visit. He's staying with my family at the villa in Positano so Alessandra and I can have our first weekend alone."

"Lucky you."

Rini had found great happiness in his marriage. Guido would give anything to feel that fulfilled. As he sat there, it came to him that he was envious of the happy-ever-after his friend Rini had achieved, a happy-ever-after Guido hadn't thought he'd wanted himself all these years.

He stared at his friend. A spirit of contentment radiated off Rini as they drove across the causeway to the Caracciolo *castello* on Posso Island that jutted into the Ionian Sea.

Only sand surrounded the ancient structure, no grass or trees. In Guido's mind, it was Italy's answer to Mont-Saint-Michel of French fame, with a benign appeal in good weather like this. But he imagined it could look quite daunting during a storm.

Guido found it fascinating to think the beautiful twin princesses of Count Onorato di Caracciolo were born and raised here, away from civilization. From this convent-like place had emerged Italy's most beautiful supermodel. One fashion cover had called Dea Loti "Italy's own Helen of Troy."

The face that launched a thousand ships had done something to Guido…

He'd been so stunned after meeting her in person that he hadn't been able to get her out of his mind. It probably wasn't a good idea to meet Rini here after all because it brought back the memory from the wedding when he'd been watching Dea, who'd been watching Rini. Was she still hungering for him? But it was too late to think about that now or wish he hadn't come. *Get a grip, Rossano.*

"You're being unusually quiet," Rini murmured as he pulled the Jeep up to the front of the castle. "I expected to see you overjoyed with your success so far."

"I am pleased," Guido muttered, "but the season isn't over yet. We've had one loss and still have some tough games to face."

Rini shut off the engine. "You've already brought your team to new heights. I'm proud of what you've done so far."

"Spoken like my best friend," Guido murmured.

He could feel Rini's eyes on him. "How is it going with your parents?"

Guido sighed. "The same. Papà is praying I'll give up this madness and come back to the company."

"Surely not right now."

"Of course not, but he fears I'll stay away from the business for good."

Rini's brow lifted. "Do *you* think you've left the shipping business for good?"

"I don't have an answer to that yet."

"Well, I'm glad you were able to break away and come. Tomorrow we'll go out on the cruiser and do some fishing. I've got some business ideas I want your opinion on. But tonight Alessandra has arranged dinner for us with one of your favorite fish dishes."

To his chagrin, Guido had a problem he couldn't talk over with Rini. How could he tell him that Rini *himself* was the problem? "I'm already salivating."

Filled with shame over his own flawed character, he jumped out of the Jeep and grabbed his gym bag that contained all he needed for this weekend visit. They walked to the front entry. When Rini opened the door, they were greeted by a marmalade cat Guido had played with at the wedding.

"Well, hello, Alfredo."

The housekeeper's pet rubbed against Guido's jean-clad leg. He put the bag down and picked him up, remembering that the cat was getting old and needed to be carried up and down stairs. "Did you know I was coming?"

Rini grinned. "He remembers you—otherwise he wouldn't let you hold him."

"I'm honored."

"Let's go up to your old room." Rini grabbed Guido's bag and they climbed the grand staircase two steps at a time past the enormous painting of

Queen Joanna to the third floor. The windows in the bedroom looked out on the sea. He'd stayed in here before the wedding. "Go ahead and freshen up, then come down to the dining room."

"I'll be right there." Still holding Alfredo, he said, "Thanks for inviting me."

Rini headed for the entry. "I've missed our talks," he said over his shoulder.

Guido watched him disappear out the door. *What in the hell is wrong with you, Rossano? No bear hug for your best friend? What has Rini ever done to you?*

He put the cat on the bed and slipped into the bathroom. When he came out, he opened his gym bag and pulled out two presents. One was a small gift he'd bought for Alessandra in Florence after a match. The other was a baby toy he'd seen in a store near his apartment. A little purple octopus with bells on the tentacles.

"We'd better not keep everyone waiting, Alfredo." He gathered the cat in his arms along with the gifts and went down the staircase to the dining room. The second he walked in, the cat took one look at Alessandra and wanted to get down. Guido lowered him to the parquet floor.

Her gaze darted to Guido and she beamed. "So that's where the cat has been! You're one of his favorite people." She rushed over to hug Guido. He hugged her back and gave her his gifts.

"You want me to open them now?"

"I think I do."

She removed the paper from the smaller box and

lifted the lid. Inside was a small enamel painting of Queen Joanna framed in gold filigree, probably three by four inches. He heard her gasp. "Oh, Guido—"

"I saw it in Florence at the House of Gold and couldn't resist. Consider it a gift to celebrate the publication of your book."

Just then Rini came in the room. *"Caro—"* she cried and rushed over to show her husband.

His friend flashed him a warm glance. "You knew exactly what she'd love."

"I read the book and was so impressed by your knowledge I had to do something to honor you."

"I'm glad you liked it. This is exquisite. I'll treasure it forever." She laid it on the hunt board and undid the large gift. "Oh, how adorable! A purple octopus! Brazzo will love it!" She gave Guido a kiss on the cheek. "Come and sit down. We want to hear all about the team and how things are going."

"First I want to hear about Brazzo."

"He's gorgeous! We'll show you videos later."

No sooner did they get settled and start to eat than Guido heard the helicopter overhead.

"That'll be my parents," Alessandra murmured as they enjoyed their meal. "They've been in Milan."

"For another of Dea's fashion shows?" Damn if the question wasn't out before he could recall it.

"Oh—I guess you didn't know that she has given up her modeling career."

Guido's fork dropped on his plate. *No more modeling?* He couldn't comprehend it. "Since when?"

"Quite a while now. She realized the life of most

supermodels fades after twenty-five years of age and it's past time for her. Dea went back to her true passion and this last year has been finishing her degree at the Accademia Roma. This is her last semester."

Her true passion? Guido blinked. He didn't know she'd ever gone to college. "I had no idea. What is she studying?"

"Period costume fashion design. I'm so thrilled for her. She has an extraordinary gift in that area."

Before Guido could think, he heard voices at the entry. Alessandra's parents walked in the room, but he only had eyes for the gorgeous woman behind them. His heart thundered.

Dea!

She wore her long hair back in a chignon, a style he hadn't seen her in. All that glossy brown hair with streaks of sunlight was hidden. The oval of her face with less makeup than he'd ever noticed before caused him to stare. With those dark burgundy eyes—like the color in a stained glass window—she was beautiful in a brand-new way.

Guido stood up and greeted the three of them. Alessandra begged her parents to join them for dinner, but they said they'd already eaten and were going upstairs.

"What about you, Dea?"

"I'd love some dinner, but first I want to see the baby. I brought Brazzo a present. I hope he doesn't have a bear yet. This one speaks!" She handed it to Alessandra, who opened it and pressed the button. They all listened and laughed.

"Brazzo will love this, but we left him with Rini's father and family. They wanted to give us a break."

"I'm sure you're thrilled, but I'm horribly disappointed."

"There'll be plenty of other times for the rest of our lives."

"You're right, of course." She sat down at the table. "I left work without grabbing a bite and now I'm starving. This dinner looks wonderful. Baked halibut and vegetables with feta cheese. How perfect!"

She was wearing a simple white blouse and a print skirt. Her outfit was so unexpectedly casual that Guido was still trying to make sense of everything when she sat down next to him.

For the rest of the meal Guido was amazed to watch her dig into her food and eat everything. Where was the woman who never ate anything that wasn't on her special diet? Come to think of it, she looked like she'd gained some becoming weight since the last time he'd seen her at the wedding.

Over a glass of wine she turned to Guido. He noticed she no longer wore her fingernails long and painted. "There's a girl at the shop named Gina. She and her fiancé, Aldo, went to the soccer game at the Stadio Emanuele last weekend."

Where was this leading?

"Aldo came in to pick Gina up and she told him I knew the owner. He fell all over me." Guido could believe that. "According to him, you were the greatest soccer player he'd ever seen and he desperately wants to meet you in person sometime, hopefully with my help."

Dea had discussed him with her coworker? He couldn't believe it.

She kept talking. "According to Aldo, the Scatto Roma team is going to win the championship this year. He was a soccer player himself, not on your level, of course. He thinks you walk on water already for lifting the B team to top-tier status."

"Thank you, Dea," he said, attempting to take it all in, but he couldn't understand her interest. "Have you ever been to a soccer match?"

"Never," she confessed without shame. "I've never even watched it on TV. You must think I'm terrible. I had no idea you'd won so many championships for Italy. Aldo said you were everyone's favorite player and the women were crazy about you."

"They were," Rini inserted with a grin.

She hadn't talked to Guido like this at the wedding reception, where she had seemed very stiff. This was something else. He decided to change the subject.

"I understand you're no longer modeling."

"Not for the last year."

"Where do you work?"

"I started at the shop of Juliana Parma ten days ago. She's *the* costume designer for the opera. I've been permitted to shadow her. My aunt Fulvia made it possible. You remember her from the wedding?"

"Of course." The woman had taken Dea away from the table before the wedding cake had been served.

"They're best friends and Juliana took me on as

a favor to my aunt. But now that I'm working there, I'm on my own and I'm terrified."

"How could you possibly be that when you've been Italy's top model?"

"That period of my life is over, and modeling modern-day fashions has nothing to do with being a period costume designer for the opera." Guido still had a hard time believing she had changed her whole life in the last year. To his mind, she was more beautiful than ever. "I have to prove myself in a whole new field. I'm not like you."

"What do you mean?"

"Alessandra said that when you bought that floundering soccer team, you had the satisfaction of being one of the greatest soccer players ever to compete in Italy. With your knowledge and confidence, you've been able to turn your team around. I'm very impressed."

"He's done that, all right," Rini concurred. "So I have an idea. Why don't the four of us go out behind the castle and play a little soccer before it gets dark? Two against two. It works even if we don't have a whole bunch of guys around. Since Brazzo was born, Alessandra and I haven't had a weekend to enjoy like this. Let's team up."

"That sounds fun!" Alessandra chimed in with enthusiasm that sounded real. "I like soccer, but I'd love to learn more about it since Rini is determined our son will be a great player like you, Guido. What do you say, Dea?"

"I'm hopeless when it comes to sports and would hate making a fool of myself, but I'll do it this once."

So she was willing to toss him a bone after she'd just admitted she'd never even seen a soccer game?

"Let me run upstairs to put on my trainers."

Alessandra patted her husband's arm. "I'll find mine too."

Rini got to his feet. "My soccer ball is around here somewhere. We'll all meet in the foyer in a few minutes."

Everyone took off except for Guido, who stood there in a funk. Since Rini's marriage, they hadn't had time to kick a ball around. And now he wanted them to play with the women?

He'd go along with this, but before he went to bed, he intended to have a talk with Rini about what was going on.

CHAPTER TWO

DEA RACED UP the stairs to her bedroom. Rini had no idea how petrified she was when it came to participating in sports. Alessandra was the one who did everything well: tennis, golf, swimming and scuba diving. But Dea didn't dare say no to his suggestion in front of Guido.

The tall, attractive dark blond was not only a recognized national celebrity in the sports field; he was Rini's best friend. Dea didn't want to be a drama queen and create a scene. Those days were relegated to the past. She'd turned over a new leaf and was embracing a different life that meant accepting challenges she'd avoided before now.

She changed out of her skirt into jeans and put on her trainers. No doubt she would fall flat on her face repeatedly for being out of her element, but at least she would be prepared. If Rini allowed her to be on his team, then she'd wouldn't feel so terrible when she let him down. Alessandra would be a much better fit for Guido when it came to sports.

How strange that today of all days Dea's folks had

come to the shop and begged her to fly home with them after work for the weekend. None of them had known that Rini and Alessandra had invited Guido. It had come as a shock to see the three of them at the dining room table.

Both on the yacht and at the wedding, Dea had only seen him dressed in a tuxedo. This evening Guido was wearing a blue polo shirt that emphasized his well-defined chest, which combined with tight jeans made it impossible to look anywhere else. Soccer kept him in the sun. His bronzed complexion accentuated the midnight blue of his dark-fringed eyes.

She could understand why female soccer fans would have gone crazy over him. Guido might not be playing soccer now, but it didn't matter. He was an incredibly appealing man.

After the fashion show on the yacht, Guido's father had sought her out. At the time she'd taken an instant dislike to the renowned shipping-company CEO. He was so full of himself that he was quite unbearable. Dea's modest father was a completely different type and so easy to be around. Meeting the puffed-up man's son was the last thing Dea and her friend Daphne, who had modeled with her, had wanted to do, but she knew she had to be gracious.

Prepared not to like his son, who was probably an obnoxious replica of his father, she'd been shocked to meet his best friend, Rini Montanari, the dark-haired handsome prince standing next to him. At that moment everything else had left her mind. He wasn't a real prince, but he'd seemed to have stepped right out of her childhood dreams. But Rini hadn't responded to her as she'd hoped and her world had fallen apart. Of course, that was ages ago...

Tonight she felt she was truly seeing Guido for the first time and not just as Rini's best friend. It had been unfair to judge him because of his father. This was important to Rini and Alessandra. For that reason she made up her mind to be a good sport and act friendly. Why not? If nothing else, she might be able to talk him into meeting Gina's fiancé after a game, or giving Aldo an autographed team poster or something.

Dea left the bedroom and hurried down to the foyer, where the others had congregated. Rini glanced at her. "While we were waiting, we flipped a coin. You're on Guido's team." He smiled broadly. "My wife is on mine."

"Hmm. I wonder how that happened. Sorry, Guido." Dea rolled her eyes at him. "You got the bad end of this deal."

"Why don't I show you a few moves before we start." He was holding the soccer ball. "Who knows what can happen?"

She chuckled. "I'm game if you are. Let's go."

They left the castle and walked around to the back, where the cruiser was pulled up to the dock in the distance. Rini and Alessandra had moved on to draw boundary lines in the sand.

While Guido explained the basic rudiments of the sport to her, there was no chitchat. He was all business. No doubt the players on his team held him in awe.

"The whole point of the game is to prevent the

other team from driving the ball forward and scor-
ing. One of the first basic moves is to take a big side
step and pull the ball with you to put space between
you and the enemy."

"Show me."

"It goes like this."

Dea watched his hard-muscled body and legs do
the move with sheer masculine grace and speed.
Whoa. She smiled. "Do that again."

He did it five more times. No matter how she an-
ticipated what he was going to do, she couldn't react
fast enough to stop him.

"Again!"

This time she was desperate to succeed. Refusing
to let him elude her, she made a flying leap and tackled him with all her strength. They both went down.
She turned over to look at him, trying to catch her
breath, but laughter kept bubbling out of her. "I'm
sorry."

"No, you're not." He lay there looking at her before bursting into laughter himself. Their faces were
so close she could tell his incredible blue eyes were
smiling. Guido Rossano was a sensational-looking
man. How could she not have noticed before today?

His gaze continued to play over her features. "For
a first soccer lesson, you did well. You'd make an excellent player in American football—tackling is what
they do in their football games. Tackling isn't what
we do in soccer. Who would have thought?"

"Forgive me. I got so frustrated I didn't know what
else to do."

"You've got all the right instincts, but you need to refine your technique to soccer or you'll get thrown out of the game."

"Hey, you two?" Rini called from a distance. "Are we going to play, or what?"

"I need to show her a few more moves before we start," Guido shouted back.

Guilt swept over her as he helped her to her feet. Conscious of their clasped hands, she eased hers from his grip. As his eyes focused on hers, her heart skipped a beat for no good reason. "We'll start with the lift, step and go." He put the ball on the ground. "Use your foot to push it toward me and watch."

Dea was loving this. She started moving the ball toward him. He lifted his foot as if to do a sideward motion. But it was a fake move. He stepped forward and drove the ball away from her. She groaned.

"Let's do that again."

She pushed the ball three more times, but he evaded her every time. "You're amazing!"

"Not amazing. I've been doing this move since childhood."

"No wonder Aldo idolizes you." After four tries she got the hang of it.

"Okay. Now what's the next move called?"

"You're not tired yet?"

"No, but maybe *you* are."

His hard jaw rose a fraction and he put his hands on his hips in a totally male stance. "This one is called the chip shot. Come toward me, moving the ball with your feet."

She did his bidding and thought he would push the ball forward, but he chipped it instead so it flipped up, catching her off guard.

"Oh! I *like* that move. I want to try it." But with her next effort, she used too much force and fell on her derriere. He chuckled and helped her to her feet.

"Try once more."

Dea did her best and stayed upright.

"Bravo. You're ready. Let's try out those moves on them before they decide they want to go home."

"You think I can do it?"

"We're about to find out." The way he smiled made him look like a devilishly handsome blond pirate with a wicked gleam in his eyes. How odd that she'd never dreamed of a tall blond pirate prince before...

The guys played goalie so the girls could battle it out. Guido hadn't had so much fun in years and was silently betting on Dea to outplay Alessandra.

Right away it became clear that Rini hadn't taught Alessandra any special moves. She could run and scrap, but Dea pulled a few moves on her with an expertise that shocked Guido. In the end, Team Scatto Roma took the honors over Team Montanari. Again he was surprised she'd caught on so quickly and he discovered he was proud of her.

Alessandra eyed the three of them. "Now it's the men's turn. You and I will play goalie, Dea."

"I'm ready."

"It's too dark out," Rini protested.

His wife smiled. "Since when has that ever stopped you? I'm counting on you to win for our side."

Guido turned to his friend. "Come on. Let's show the girls how the game is played."

"You're on."

Before they spread out, Guido took Dea aside. "Try not to let the ball get past you. Do whatever you need to do."

"I'm afraid Rini will kick it so hard I won't stand a chance, but I'll try."

He squeezed her elbow. "No one can ask for more than that."

In a minute play commenced. Rini gave as good as he got, but Guido's competitive spirit had kicked in. That's when he realized he was fighting a demon from the past and taking it out on his friend. The score was two to two. Rini went all out for the last play. He gave the ball a kick as fierce as the expression on his face. Dea didn't stand a chance. Or so Guido thought until he saw her catch it midair.

"I did it!" she cried out in unfeigned excitement. Forgetting everything, he ran toward her and swung her around. "Keep this up and I'll sign you on to my team." Before he lowered her warm beautiful body to the ground, there was a breathless moment when even in the semidark her cognac eyes seemed to sparkle. He wanted badly to taste her mouth, but they had an audience and she would probably slap his face.

Alessandra ran up to Dea and hugged her. "I thought you said you've never done sports. What's happened?"

Dea flicked Guido a glance. "I had a good teacher."

"I'll say you did. Come on. Let's go in."

Rini kissed his wife. "We'll catch up with you two in a minute."

As the women walked off, Guido sucked in his breath. The time for the talk with Rini had come. His friend stared him down. "Do you want to tell me what's going on with you? Everything has been different since Alessandra and I have been married, so I'll make this easier for you and start. Why haven't you wanted to get together like we used to do?"

He rubbed the back of his neck. "You really don't know?"

"Guido—" The bleak expression on his face spoke volumes and made Guido feel guiltier than ever. "Talk to me! If I've done something wrong, I'll fix it if I can."

"You can't."

"Why?"

It was hard to swallow. "I'm ashamed to tell you."

"Why?" he demanded again.

Just tell him, Rossano, and get it over with.

"It's ever since that night on the yacht. I'd never known jealousy in my life until then. But I did the moment I met Dea and she took one look at you and fell head over heels."

Rini's black brows formed a line above his dark eyes. "Way back then *you* were jealous of *that*?"

"The force of it hit me like a blow to my gut."

"Are you telling me you were interested in Dea?" He shook his head in total bewilderment. "I thought you'd never met her before that night."

"I hadn't, but her face was continually in the news. Seeing her on deck did something visceral to me. But before I could do anything about it, she walked right into your arms."

Rini shook his head. "I don't know what to say."

"You don't have to say anything. You couldn't help that she was attracted to you. The fact that I knew you weren't attracted to her didn't help me. I've suffered ever since that night because I've held something against you that couldn't possibly have been your fault. You have every right to tell me to go to hell and stay there."

Rini came closer. "That's the last thing I want to do. All this time you've been suffering…"

"And I've made *you* suffer. I'm so sorry, Rini."

To his shock, his friend smiled. "If I don't miss my guess, I believe cupid shot an arrow into your heart when you laid eyes on Dea. The same thing happened to me when I met Alessandra."

"You're right," he murmured.

"*Paisano*—you've been smitten since the night your father brought Dea and her friend over to meet us after the fashion show. After your experience with Carla, I've wondered for years when love would hit you. Little does your *papà* know his endless machinations to find you a wife finally worked!"

Guido threw his head back. "They did."

"Now that I know your secret, I understand what happened out here on the sand just now. You swung Dea around with more energy than I've ever seen in you. I guess her flying tackle earlier had something to do with your reaction."

"I've never been so surprised in my life."

Rini grinned. "Contact sports can be fun, especially when it was Dea who initiated that move. You must be doing something right or she wouldn't have allowed herself to get in *your* arms."

No one ever had a better friend. Guido cocked his head. "You don't despise me for being a total fool this last year?"

"It's forgotten." He gripped Guido's shoulder. "Listen—I'm going to tell you a secret and I hope you can handle it. You have no idea the number of times I envied you for all the women who threw themselves at you. I didn't have that experience growing up and feared I'd never meet the right woman for me.

"Need I remind you of Arianna, who was so crazy about you she came to every game and hung around you for weeks? I might as well have been invisible. She was gorgeous and I was jealous as hell."

"You're kidding—"

"No. Don't you remember my telling you that I wouldn't have minded if she'd come after me, but it didn't happen? And then there was Carla." Guido preferred not to think about her. "Let's be honest. You could have had any woman you ever wanted."

"Except Dea...who wanted you."

His dark brows lifted. "Dea didn't want me. We talked about it. Growing up in a castle together, she and Alessandra had this idea of marrying a tall, dark-haired prince. My image filled the bill. But that's all it was. The image vanished. If you're asking me if she still sees me as her prince, the answer is a definite no. Surely you could tell that at the wedding. I'm now her irritating brother-in-law."

"She seemed to be in a world of her own that day," Guido said.

"That's because she was going through a major life crisis, another thing you're going through yourself taking on a soccer team. In many ways, you and Dea are a lot alike. You had your pick of women over the years but didn't settle. She always had her pick of men, yet didn't end up with any of them. One day she's going to fall so hard that'll be it. Lucky will be the man who captures her heart."

"Wouldn't it be funny if it turned out to be me," he muttered.

Rini shot him a piercing glance. "You and I both know that no matter how bad it looks, you never leave the stadium until the game is over. Astounding surprises happen in the last second."

"True." Guido couldn't argue with that kind of logic. Nor could he doubt that Rini had given him all the truth inside him.

His friend picked up the ball. "Come on. Let's get back to the *castello*. How soon do you have to return to Rome?"

"I have to fly out early Sunday morning for the game."

"I happen to know Dea will be around until then too. Alessandra had planned a day out on the cruiser for the three of us tomorrow. But with Dea still here, it'll be even more fun. Maybe you can teach her how to water ski. She gave up after trying it the first time."

"She hasn't done any water sports?" Guido was incredulous.

"A little swimming. That's it. But the way she got into the soccer match proves to me she's not only game, she's a fast learner. I only have one question. Are *you* game?"

Until their talk a few minutes ago Guido would have said no.

They returned to the castle, where the girls had dessert and coffee waiting for them in the dining room. Guido enjoyed the snack while they chuckled about Dea's tackle, then he excused himself to go up to bed.

"Don't forget tomorrow," Rini called after him. "Once we've eaten breakfast, we'll go out on the cruiser."

"Sounds good." With a smile for the three of them, he left the room.

Alessandra came to Dea's bedroom the next morning in order to French-braid her hair before breakfast.

"Thanks for doing this for me. I can't do it right. Now it won't get in my face."

"As you know, I had mine cut short years ago because I spent so much time in the water scuba diving."

"I'm thinking I might get mine cut too, after I get back to Rome."

"Oh, no, Dea. Your gorgeous long hair? Are you sure?"

"It drives me insane while I'm working. I used to wonder why Juliana wore her hair short. Now I know. Hair gets in the way when you're kneeling in front of a mannequin to work on a hem. We're constantly bending over to examine a drawing or a cut of fabric. All you need is an irritating strand to fall at a critical moment."

"Well, it's your call," Alessandra murmured. "Now let's hurry down to breakfast before the guys eat everything in sight."

"I just hope Guido's forgiven me for tackling him. I don't know what came over me."

"I do. It's called frustration beyond bearing! They're both so good at everything it can drive you crazy! I'm sure no one ever did such a thing to Guido before."

"That's what has me worried."

"Rini laughed about it after we went to bed. He's sure you're the only woman who ever got the best of Guido."

"Now I'm worried he'll pull something on *me* today."

Alessandra's eyes sparkled. "Just don't let your guard down." Her warning excited Dea.

After her sister left the bedroom, she dressed in shorts and a yellow top worn over her orange-and-white-striped bikini. Once ready, she grabbed her tote bag and flew down the stairs in sandals to the dining room. At the entrance, a pair of inky-blue eyes met hers across the room, causing her pulse to race.

"*Buongiorno*, Dea." His deep voice curled through to her insides.

This morning Guido had put on a white T-shirt

and cargo pants that couldn't hide his powerful legs. He held a mug of coffee and looked so sensational she was taken back. A nervous smile broke out on her face. "I hope you didn't wake up with any aches or pains."

"I'm managing to survive," he mocked gently.

Uh-oh. "Where is everyone?"

"Alessandra grabbed a jam *cornetto* and went out to help Rini load the cruiser. Come and join me before we head out."

Since Guido was still here, maybe it meant he'd been waiting for her. Her heart flipped over again.

"Cook makes the best cappuccino in the world."

"I agree," he murmured over the rim of his cup.

Aware of his scrutiny, she walked over to the hunt board and reached for a pastry. After pouring herself coffee, she moved to the table to eat. Once he joined her, she couldn't resist asking, "Are you a champion water-skier too? Alessandra said Rini can't wait to get out on the water and ski double with you."

He sat back in the chair, studying her through shuttered eyes. "I've done a little of everything."

"But soccer is your passion."

"One of them."

A shiver of excitement ran through her. The intimation of what his other passions might be brought heat to her cheeks. With his dark blond hair slightly disheveled, she discovered he had a potent male appeal no woman could possibly ignore. His girlfriends must be legion.

Once they'd finished breakfast, they left the castle for the dock around the back. During their short walk she thought about him and Rini being such close friends since childhood. They were so different, *except* in two major ways. Their masculine charisma was lethal and they both had an air of authority that seemed to be part of their natures.

Dea had met many men over the years, but none of them possessed those extraordinary qualities. She might have known that Rini's best man would be someone who stood out from all the rest too. He wasn't anything like his father. At least she didn't think so, but what did she know?

Maybe if she'd stayed at the table the night of the wedding reception and had gotten better acquainted with the head of Rossano Shipping Lines, she'd have seen similarities that hadn't been apparent at first. Guido was his son after all.

In the past Dea had had a problem with making snap judgments about people. It came from a fear that people saw her as only a superficial narcissist—an unfair label given to models in general. Her mother had pointed out that she put up a defensive shield because part of her felt insecure. Dea had had to learn to give everyone a chance.

Since she'd gone back to school, she'd been making a conscious effort to get along with people. While she and Gina had been at the shop discussing one of the designs that wasn't working, she'd learned the other woman loved the theater. Dea would never have guessed that—all Gina seemed to talk about was Aldo, who lived in her apartment building.

He worked in a garage and wasn't happy because he couldn't make good money. The last thing he'd do was spend the little he had on going to watch a play he had no interest in. Soccer was a different story. Dea had offered to go to the theater with Gina, who was delighted. They planned to see *Othello* at the Silvano Toti Globe in Rome the next weekend. It would give them a chance to study the costuming while they enjoyed Shakespeare.

"Hey, you two," Rini called to them.

When they reached the cabin cruiser, Dea climbed over the side first. After stowing her tote bag below deck, she came back up and slipped on the life belt Alessandra handed her.

Rini took the wheel and signaled to Guido, who untied the ropes. Dea drew in a deep breath, filled with a sense of anticipation that was new to her. She wouldn't lie to herself. Guido's presence was the reason for this feeling, plus a warm sun that portended a perfect day to be out on the water.

Except for a few freighters way off in the distance, they had the sea to themselves. Five minutes later Rini cut the engine. He shot Guido a glance. The other man had already removed his T-shirt. The sight of his hard-muscled body changed the tenor of Dea's breathing.

"Ready to give the girls a show?"

Guido fastened his life belt. "Whenever you are."

The guys tossed two slalom skis in the water and dove off the transom like porpoises. Alessandra turned to Dea. "While I drive, you get in the back.

Keep an eye on the ropes while they're uncoiling. When the guys are up, spot them. In case they get into any trouble, tell me and I'll cut the engine."

With a legitimate excuse to feast her eyes on Guido, she knelt on the banquette and watched them fasten their skis. Then she heard Rini yell, "Hit it!" Alessandra increased the speed and a minute later both men were out of the water like professionals who'd been doing this for years.

They moved in wide arcs and displayed an expertise on one ski Dea marveled over. How would it be to ski like that? "They're fabulous!" she called to Alessandra. "Have you gotten up on one ski yet?"

"No. It's hard."

I want to learn.

Several minutes went by before she saw Rini lift his free arm. "I think they want to stop," she shouted.

"Okay! Start reeling in the ropes and coil them."

Dea did as she asked and wound the rope. Alessandra brought the cruiser around and cut the engine in order to reach for the skis and put them on the transom. With masculine dexterity, the men heaved themselves aboard. Dea couldn't take her eyes off Guido. The sun bathed him in light. He looked like a golden god as he reached for a towel.

"Bravo," she told both of them.

Rini flicked her a glance. "Think you want to do it?"

She finished coiling the second rope. "I'd like to try, but it won't be on one ski. Can you do it on your feet?"

Deep laughter came out of Guido. "I'm afraid it hurts too much."

"Even though you were a soccer player?"

"Even though. Want to go now?"

No...but she *had* to. That was her new rule. Don't hang back. She'd given up before when she'd gone skiing with Alessandra, but her sister was so good at it that Dea had decided not to try anymore. Thank goodness she'd worked out in a gym close to her apartment all these years in order to stay in shape.

"Sure."

"Good for you. There's very little wind right now. It's the best time."

Rini nodded. "I'll drive and Alessandra will spot you."

"Okay," she said on a jerky breath. *Here goes nothing.* Dea undid the belt in order to remove her clothes, then refastened it.

Guido told her to walk over so he could fit her feet in the skis and adjust them. While he hunkered down, she put a hand on his solid shoulder to steady herself. The warmth from his skin crept into her body. Then she stepped out of the skis with his help.

"I'll go first." He jumped in the water and she handed him the skis. Then it was her turn. Once her head surfaced she felt Guido's hands steady her from behind while Rini started the cruiser and slowly pulled away from them. Alessandra let out the rope.

"Grasp it in your hand while I put the skis on you." Guido did everything with ease. "Now I want you to lie back in my arms and brace your legs so they're ready to come out of the water straight. Don't be frightened. When I call out, 'Hit it,' you'll be pulled right up. Just hold on to the rope with both hands. Let the boat do the rest and don't look down. I'll be right here in case you fall."

"Thank you." Saying a little prayer, she watched until the rope was all the way out. Suddenly she heard Guido's voice and the cruiser leaped forward. To her shock she rose right up on top of the water and was skimming across the placid surface.

Dea couldn't believe she was actually water-skiing again, but she was moving fast and made the mistake of doing the one thing Guido had told her not to do. That's when she lost her balance and let go of the rope. The boat swung around and came alongside her. In a second Guido was there and pulled her back against his chest.

"You were terrific."

"No. I blew it because I looked down."

Her sister smiled at her from the boat. "I didn't get up until four tries."

"Let's do it again," Guido urged her. "Your skis are still on. Throw her the rope, Alessandra, and we'll have another go."

Uh-oh. But she refused to reveal weakness in front of Guido.

Once again Rini sat at the wheel and started the engine while Guido put her in the same position as before. He tugged her braid. "Did you know you have a lethal weapon here?"

"I'm sorry if it flipped you."

"I'll live."

His comment brought a giggle out of her, but it was

lost in a cry when she felt the cruiser take off and pull her on top of the water. More used to the sensation, she stayed up rather inelegantly for over a minute, but her legs were tired because she wasn't used to this.

She lifted her arm and immediately Rini cut the engine. This time when she sank in the water, she didn't panic like before. The belt helped her stay afloat. This was fun. So much fun she couldn't believe she'd lived twenty-eight years without knowing the thrill.

CHAPTER THREE

DEA HAD HEARD the others talking about planning a scuba diving trip. She didn't know if she could ever gird up her courage to take lessons and try it, but she wouldn't say no if she got the chance. That was because she had an excellent teacher in Guido, who was fast approaching. The glint of admiration in those dark blue eyes mesmerized her.

"We'll have you on one ski before the day is out."

"Not now. Two are all I can handle, but one day I plan to get there."

After Guido removed her skis, Rini helped her onto the transom and Alessandra was there to hand her a towel.

Now it was Alessandra's turn to ski while Guido spotted her. Dea let out the rope and watched her sister come out of the water on two skis like a champion.

No longer envious of her sister, she admired her. Once Alessandra had done a four-minute run, they brought her in. Dea praised her sister. As for the adoring look in Rini's eyes, it was something to behold. To be loved like that...

For the next hour they enjoyed an alfresco lunch and spent the rest of the day swimming around the boat and fishing with different lures. Dea had gone trolling with her parents many times in the past, so this wasn't new to her. But the company made it an experience she didn't want to end. Guido and Rini exchanged fishing stories and past shenanigans that had the girls roaring with laughter.

They arrived back at the castle having caught a lot of sun and enough cod to feed everyone, including their parents. The cook grilled it for their dinner. Alessandra and Dea helped in the kitchen to speed up the process for all of them, and they sat down to a delicious meal.

In time they retreated to the dayroom, where her father got out the family movies and turned on the TV screen. "First we'll watch the latest videos of Brazzo."

Alfredo wandered in and climbed on her lap. She hugged the cat to her.

The videos of the baby were adorable. Then her father put in another video.

"This shows you girls playing house with your own play castle when you were six."

Dea had forgotten about that one. They used to set it up in the living room with all kinds of props, dolls and clothes. She and Alessandra wore long make-shift costumes and performed as if they were doing a documentary.

"This is where Dea's dream to become a costume designer began," her father informed them. "She was the one to decide what they would wear."

"I was so bossy it's embarrassing."

Her father smiled. "If you'll notice, Alessandra was much more interested in the boat outside the castle she moved around and around."

Everyone laughed, but Dea was mortified. She hoped the videos would end soon. Dea's prayers were answered when her father finally shut off the TV and her parents went to bed. Then Rini and Alessandra said good-night, leaving her alone with Guido. Her heart beat fast.

"I've enjoyed getting to know you today, Dea. Since we're both working in Rome, I'd like to spend time with you again."

"I had a fun time too, and would like that."

"Then I'll call you later in the week. Much as I'd love to stay up and talk to you longer, I've got to get to bed. I have a big game tomorrow and have to be up early."

"Of course. Good luck. I'm counting on your team to win."

"Thank you. So am I." He got to his feet. Alfredo leaped off her lap to follow him.

"No, no, Alfredo." She jumped up and grabbed him. "You have to go to your own bed." Dea lifted her head to look at Guido. "Good night."

His eyes pierced hers. *"Buonanotte."*

Dea took the cat back to the housekeeper's suite, then went upstairs.

After a luxurious shower, she reached for the laptop and climbed into bed to search for the Scatto Roma website. A world of revelation met her eyes.

For the next hour she was entranced and read every bit of information about the history of the team, the new owner, the players, schedules, stats, the soccer museum and the online store.

When she typed in Guido's name, dozens of references came up. There were galleries of his pictures from when he'd been the sensational soccer player of the day. They called him *Cuor di Leone*, the Lionhearted. The explanation stated that it wasn't in honor of Richard the Lionheart but for Guido's father, Leonides Rossano, who was known as Naples's business lion.

Every picture of the striking, fierce competitor took her breath. Guido had worn his hair longer then. In some pictures it resembled a lion's coloring. She went back to the online shop and picked out two large signed posters of him to be sent to her. One was for Gina to give Aldo.

The other poster she'd keep in the bedroom at her apartment. Dea had never been a typical teen who worshipped boys and musical groups. She'd never had posters on her bedroom walls. This would be her first one.

Because of her insecurities, Dea had never handled boys right at school. Since becoming a model, she could never trust the men she dated to see past her looks. Therapy had taught her she hadn't given them a chance. There'd probably been several great guys she might have fallen in love with if she'd understood herself better.

With a deep sigh, she put the laptop on the floor

and got under the covers, but she didn't fall asleep for a long time. Her mind relived those moments in the water when Guido had cradled her in his arms. He smelled wonderful and made her feel safe and confident enough to move beyond the tight boundaries she'd drawn for herself years ago. She'd see him at breakfast before he left. Morning couldn't come soon enough.

At eight the next day she went down to the dining room and found her parents eating. "*Buongiorno*, darling."

She kissed their cheeks. "Where's everyone else?"

"Your sister and Rini drove Guido to the airport two hours ago."

"Two hours ago?" Dea was shocked.

"He had to get back early for the game. The two of them will be back later."

With the disappointing news that he'd already gone, the bottom fell out of her day. "I have to get back to Rome too."

"But your flight won't leave until three. Sit down and eat breakfast with us. We know we're lucky you would come home with us this weekend. Have you had a good time so far?"

"It's been great." That was the truth.

She poured herself some coffee. Guido had told her he'd phone her. She hoped he meant it. There'd been moments this weekend when she'd thought he was attracted to her, but she'd learned from her sister that Guido had enjoyed his share of girlfriends.

He was her brother-in-law's age, thirty-two, yet

still not engaged or married. Maybe he was this way around all women, making them feel special in the moment without having deeper feelings for them. He couldn't have known she'd be coming to the *castello*. Was he glad to discover she'd come? Would he forget about calling her once he was back in Rome?

A tiny moan escaped. There she went again, making this whole situation about her. He'd said he would phone. But until he did, she had work to do. Her mind cast back to what her mother had told her when she was at her lowest ebb. *One day your prince will find you. In the meantime, work on finding yourself.*

Good advice. *Keep remembering it, Dea. Hit the gym before work and concentrate on the fabulous opportunity of learning from the great Juliana.*

Guido waited until Wednesday morning to phone Rini and Alessandra to thank them for the great weekend.

"Are you telling me you had a better time than you'd imagined?"

"You could say that." Thoughts of Dea had been on his mind ever since. "Before I went to bed that night, I told Dea I'd call her, but I don't have her cell phone number."

"I've got it."

Guido wrote it down. "Thanks for that."

"You're welcome. Congratulations on another win on Sunday. Your name is all over the sports news."

"We're on a roll right now. Here's hoping it lasts."

"I have no doubt of it."

"Thanks again for everything. Talk to you soon."

"Ciao."

At noon Guido phoned Dea, but his call was put through to her voice mail. He wanted to meet her for lunch on Thursday if she was available and asked her to call him back. Later in the day Dea rang back. They decided on a little bistro around the corner near her work. She'd meet him there tomorrow at twelve thirty. With the opera's opening coming up in May, they were swamped with work.

Thursday finally arrived. Guido had been living for it. Even in jeans and a top with her hair pulled back in a chignon, Dea was a standout beauty. She drew the attention of everyone when she walked in the foyer, but no one more than Guido, who'd arrived ten minutes ahead of time to wait for her.

A smile lit up her face. "Hi, Guido! I hope I'm not too late."

"I'm early," he explained. "Shall we eat outside?"

"I'd love it. The workrooms tend to suffocate you when we're all in there running around for this and that."

The waiter showed them to a table and they sat down while he took their order. "I'm glad I called ahead for a table. This place is crowded."

She nodded. "It's so popular I've only been here once. And that time we had to wait in line for a half hour, which made us late for work."

"Us?"

"My friend Gina, who works at the shop too. I told you about her. By the way, congratulations on your win last Sunday. You must be feeling on top of the world."

"That feeling lasted until Monday morning."

She chuckled. "So your fears are working up to a frenzy again for this coming Sunday?"

"*Frenzy* is the right word."

Their pasta arrived. "While the waiter is here, would you like some wine?"

"Not during my workday, thank you. Just coffee."

"You're no fun."

"It wouldn't be so funny if I designed the skinny pants for the baritone and they ended up being for the fat tenor, who couldn't pull them on."

Guido burst into laughter. "I see where you're going with this. You've made your case."

Dea was working her charm on him and it made him nervous as hell, but he couldn't identify the reason why until after she'd told him she had to get right back to work. He followed her through the restaurant to the front door.

"Thanks for lunch, Guido. I enjoyed this break with you."

"So did I. I'll phone you again."

"Good. Ciao."

He watched her walk off. So did every other male in sight, many of whom had probably recognized the famous supermodel.

On the drive back to his apartment, he figured out what was wrong with him. Dea wasn't just any woman. She had the title of princess, if she ever wanted to use it, but he couldn't see her doing that.

What worried him was that she'd become his addiction since their unexpected time at the castle. He knew he wanted a serious relationship with her, but would a princess consider what he did for a living to be something suitable?

Guido's father had always been very negative about soccer being a proper career. The comments he had made in the past were never very far from the surface, and they came back to haunt Guido now. For the next few days he let that concern prevent him from calling Dea again.

On Saturday afternoon Guido was getting ready to leave the stadium and found Sergio in the mail room. "How come you're still here?"

"I've had to stay open until the suppliers delivered this week's inventory. A few more orders need to get mailed out before I go to my sister's place for a party."

"That sounds fun. Before I leave, tell me, what's selling the most?"

"Besides T-shirts, our signed soccer balls and autographed posters of our team's stars, of course. We can't keep in enough of the ones of Drago and Dante."

That figured. The two forwards were the current rage. Guido's brows lifted. "How many requests came in for posters of you?"

"Give it up, Guido. None this week, but last weekend someone ordered two posters of you. They picked the one of you making the point that won our game against Team Lancio. I blinked when I saw the name."

"Why?"

"How many women do you know with the name

Dea? You know who I'm talking about. Italy's own Helen of Troy."

Guido's heartbeat skidded off the charts. "I imagine there are hundreds of Deas living in Italy," he muttered in a gravelly voice. Sergio knew nothing about Guido's private life.

"You're probably right."

"Don't keep your family waiting. I'll see you tomorrow before the game."

"Ciao, boss."

He left the stadium and went out to the parking lot for his car. Tonight his parents had invited him for dinner at the family villa in Naples. He'd take the helicopter from the airport.

During the flight he couldn't stop thinking about Dea. It had to be a coincidence that someone with the same name had ordered from the store. Much as he wished he could forget it, he remained preoccupied throughout the evening with his parents. It was good to see them, but he was anxious to get back to Rome before it grew too late.

After his return, he had every intention of driving straight to his apartment. But at the last second he turned off the main route and headed for the stadium. He wouldn't be able to sleep until he knew who had ordered those posters.

The night watchman nodded to him before he let himself inside the store. Once on the computer, he found the week's invoices and scrolled down until he saw a name and address near the bottom that stood out like a flashing red light. *Dea Caracciolo, Via Giustiniani 2, Roma, Italia.*

She'd ordered them the previous Saturday night.

The breath Guido had been holding escaped. That exclusive, pricey address was near the Pantheon, not far from the soccer stadium. She'd ordered two posters of him. He remembered her telling him about her friend Gina, whose fiancé, Aldo, wanted to meet him. Maybe Dea had decided to buy her a signed poster of Guido to give to him. But why had she ordered two?

Guido walked through to the mail room. No tubes or packaged soccer balls were in the out basket. That meant Sergio had taken all the mail to the post office on his way home. She would have received them by now.

The worry he'd felt since their lunch was suddenly replaced by a flicker of hope that his job didn't turn her off. But ordering some posters from the store could mean anything. Guido would be a fool to jump to conclusions until he saw her again.

If he hadn't stopped in to talk to Sergio for a minute, he would never have known she'd ordered something from the store. Every Italian male was halfway in love with Dea's image. It was no surprise his business partner had picked up on her name immediately.

Preoccupied with thoughts of her, he locked up and drove home to his apartment. Morning would come early—he would be meeting with the team and the coaches then. The game against Genoa tomorrow would be critical. Granted, his team had been riding a wave since last November with only one loss, but

that could change. A defeat at this stage would tell
the soccer world that Team Scatto Roma wasn't ready
to compete at A-tier status.

Five more games to go. The season would be over
at the end of May. Tonight his father had asked him
if he intended to continue for a second season. Guido
couldn't give him an answer, but he'd promised to
work part-time at the shipping office during June and
July. That was as much as he could agree to and still
run summer-camp training sessions with the team.

There were other businessmen who would love to
buy him out if the team won the national B championship at the end of May. But the decision to sell was
still a long way off. Going back to the shipping firm
full-time meant signing on as CEO. Guido wasn't
ready for that. At the moment he loved the work he
was doing. Whether that translated into being fully
involved in the soccer world for the rest of his life
was a question he couldn't answer yet.

When he'd made the decision to buy a failing team,
some element in his life had been missing. It was still
missing. The more he thought about it, the more he
feared that no matter what path he took, his life would
go on to be unfulfilling without the right woman.

Now that he'd spent some time with a Dea he
hadn't known existed, the truth of that statement
stood out as nothing else could have. He'd lived with
her image for a long time, but with that tackle, she'd
gotten under his skin in a brand-new way. There was
a fire in her he wanted, needed to explore.

Guido fell into bed experiencing alternate waves of

anxiety and excitement at the thought of being with her again. He needed to call her but couldn't handle falling so hard for her only to meet with eventual rejection because his choice of career didn't meet her expectations.

If those posters had been ordered for her friend only, then he didn't want to know about it.

Stadio Emanuele held seventy thousand fans. Dea had researched everything on the website before hiring a taxi to drop her off Sunday afternoon. Tickets for the game against the soccer team from Genoa were still available, but she had to get to the ticket office two hours before the match started.

She'd never been to a sporting event. Men, women, children of all ages made up the massive crowd. They were fired up and so noisy already she could hardly hear herself think. This was sheer craziness.

After standing in line for twenty minutes, it was her turn. She asked for the best ticket on the long side—as if she knew what she was talking about—and was charged 130 euros. Before she went to her seat, she wanted to visit the soccer museum, but she found out it would be open for only fifteen more minutes.

She had to wait to get inside, but by the time she reached the doors, the person in charge announced the museum was closing. If people wanted to see pictures and videos of the all-time best Italian soccer greats, they would have to come another day. People filed out.

Dea stood aside until the last one had gone. "Signor? When will you be open again?"

"Tomorrow afternoon."

"Until how late?"

"Seven o'clock."

"I'll come after I get off work." She wanted to see videos of Guido that couldn't be viewed anywhere else.

The attractive Italian in charge gave her a long look of male admiration and approached her. He'd probably been a soccer player himself, but she noticed he had a very slight limp. "I've seen you before, signorina. You're Dea the model, aren't you?"

Uh-oh. "How did you know?"

He let out a hearty laugh. "Surely you are joking." His hand went over his heart. "Your pictures are on the inside of half the locker doors in the gym here at the stadium."

Heat rushed to her cheeks. "I think you're full of it, but thank you for the compliment. Now I'd better get going and find my seat before the match begins, but I'll be back."

"You're here alone?"

"Yes."

"Is this your first time at the stadium?"

"Yes."

"Be careful. It can get rowdy out there during a game."

"I've heard, but I can take care of myself."

He grinned. "I'll look for you tomorrow."

She thanked him, then left the store to make her way through the crowds to her seat.

The next two hours felt like being on a giant roller-coaster ride, taking her emotions up and down. She'd never sat through anything so riveting. Many times she saw those few moves Guido had taught her. They helped her understand the game a little because she'd been taught by a master. Her admiration for him grew seeing his team play like this.

To her chagrin, the score remained tied until the last few seconds, when Guido's team had a break-through by the crowd favorite Dante. When his kick got past the goalie, the crowd let out a deafening roar. Everyone went wild over the two–one score, scream-ing, "Dante! Dante!"

Dea was elated for Guido, but she barely escaped the pandemonium inside the stadium with her life. Thank goodness she'd arranged for a taxi ahead of time to meet her outside. Otherwise she would have been forced to walk blocks.

She asked the driver to stop at a deli so she could take food home to eat. Later, after getting comfort-able on the couch, she watched the ten o'clock news. The sports segment featured a clip of the soccer game. She heard the announcer praise the rise of the Scatto Roma team and pictures of Dante were flashed on the screen. Guido had to be so proud.

After working up some new costume sketches for tomorrow, she went to bed and got up early to go to the gym before reporting to the shop for work. The costumes for *Don Giovanni* were shaping up. She worked hard and didn't lift her head until five thirty.

Though she'd planned to go to the stadium museum after work this evening, she changed her mind. If she ran into Guido by mistake, he wouldn't believe it was a mistake.

The man who worked at the soccer museum had recognized her on Sunday, and she realized he had to be a friend of Guido's. She should have disguised herself. If he happened to mention that she'd been in the museum, Guido would suspect she'd been looking for him.

Because he hadn't phoned her since their lunch, that was the last thing she wanted him to think. *Let your prince find you.*

By Thursday she was totally deflated that Guido hadn't tried to reach her. At the end of work she found Gina and handed her a tube. "I have a present for Aldo."

"What?"

"Open the end and see."

Gina did her bidding and pulled out the signed poster of a twenty-year-old Guido caught in action midair with the banner *Cuor di Leone*. "Oh, Dea—" She lifted shining eyes to her. "Aldo's going to be thrilled when I give him this."

Dea had been just as thrilled when she opened her own tube and spread the poster on her bed. It now graced her bedroom wall. How she would have loved to meet the dashing athlete back then!

"I'm sorry it was already signed when it was printed."

"That doesn't matter. Isn't he gorgeous? Of course, I don't dare tell Aldo that."

"That might be wise." No man compared to Guido.

"You're fantastic, Dea!" She put the poster down and hugged her so hard she almost knocked her over. "How much do I owe you?"

"Nothing. I wanted to do this for you."

"Ooh." She squealed. "I'm so glad work is over. I'm going to drive by the garage and surprise him with it. You're the best friend I ever had."

Dea watched her run out of the shop. It had made her glad to see her new friend this happy. While she was cleaning up a few minutes later, the middle-aged receptionist came in the back room.

"Dea? There's a man here to see you."

Her heartbeat picked up. She lifted her head. "Did he give you his name?"

"He only said he'd come from the museum at the Stadio Emanuele."

Museum? How had the man running it found out she worked here? "Please tell him I'll be right out."

Most everyone had left already. She hurried into the ladies' room to freshen up and make sure the clip holding her chignon in place was still secure. Her uniform was a pair of sneakers, jeans and a top. Today she'd worn a simple red tee with short sleeves.

She went back in the room for her purse and made her way through the shop past all the racks of costumes to the reception area. Her footsteps slowed. Instead of the dark-haired man from the museum, she spied the dark blond male who'd been haunting her dreams. He stood in front of a dozen framed photographs of Juliana taken at various operas.

Dressed in beige chinos and a silky black shirt with an open collar and short sleeves, his tall, well-honed physique captured her gaze. She couldn't look anywhere else. "Guido?" she asked in a breathless voice. Dea had feared he might never call her again.

He turned to her. Those midnight blue eyes raked over her from head to toe, spilling warmth through her body. "I'm glad I caught you before you left," he said in his deep voice. "My business partner and former soccer buddy Sergio Colombo told me you were going to come by the museum on Monday. When you didn't show, I'm afraid he was very disappointed."

Her brows met in a delicate frown. "I don't understand."

"When an order for two posters came in online, he was the one who sent them out to a Dea Caracciolo. As soon as you walked in the museum, he recognized you as the famous model and made the connection. You're all he could talk about. Surely you know you made a conquest of him?"

After being in therapy, she didn't like that word anymore. Was this all about Sergio? "He was very nice and warned me to be careful in case the crowd got too boisterous."

"He is nice, but he's become supersensitive since his divorce. Why didn't you come?"

"Please tell him I had to work later than planned." Guido probably saw through her lie, but she wasn't about to tell him the truth.

He moved closer with his hands on his hips. The tension was thick between them. "Did you enjoy the soccer match Sunday?"

"I loved it, actually. Even with the few moves you taught me, I was able to understand some of it and enjoy it. Congratulations on your win. My ears rang with Dante's name all the way home in the taxi."

A glimmer of a smile hovered at one corner of his compelling mouth. He cocked his head. "I was in the dugout. But if I'd known you wanted to see a match, you could have sat in my suite to watch it."

"I should think the last thing the owner of the team would want is to worry about entertaining a guest while you're invested in an important game like that one."

"It depends on the guest. Why didn't you just call and ask me to send you a couple of posters?"

She sucked in her breath. "I didn't want to impose on you. It was easy enough to go online. They were for my friend."

"So I gathered. Now that we have matters clarified, the reason I'm here is to ask you out to dinner. If you come with me, you'll win my forgiveness for being ignominiously tackled. You owe me that much."

Another rush of heat swept through her. Looking at his virile physique now, she couldn't believe she'd done such a thing. "I'll never live it down."

"I won't hold it against you forever," he drawled in a seductive tone. "Do you have plans for this evening?"

"No," she answered honestly. "I intended to go

home for a meal and watch a little television before going to bed."

"You like TV?"

"A good film is one of my guilty pleasures."

"Can you give it a miss long enough to spend the evening with me?"

Thump, thump went her heart. The last time she'd seen him was at the bistro. But her fear that she'd never see him again had vanished because he was standing right here in front of her. Dea wanted to get to know him better and this was her chance.

"I'd like that very much, but I'll need to go home first and change."

"*Bene.* I'll drive you."

"I have my own car."

"Then I'll follow and wait for you in front of your apartment."

At this point he probably knew exactly where she lived. "My car is parked in the alley around the corner. It won't take me long."

"That's good. Plan to wear whatever you like."

Dea felt feverish with anticipation as she drove to her apartment. In the rearview mirror she could see Guido behind the wheel of a sleek black Lamborghini.

She pulled into the private parking area and hurried up to her apartment. Since he wore casual attire, she didn't want to be overdressed. After a quick shower, she put on a silky thin-striped shirtdress in tan and cream with a drawstring at the waist and a curved shirttail hem. The sleeves fell to the elbow, a classic look. She teamed a pearl clip that held her hair in place with a small pair of pearl earrings.

Once she'd slipped on tan heels, she applied lipstick and felt ready. When she left the apartment and approached his car waiting at the entrance, she trembled to think this fabulous man wanted to be with her this evening.

He levered himself from the driver's seat and opened the door for her. She felt his gaze play over her as she got inside. "You look stunning," he murmured near her cheek. His breath sent rivulets of delight through her.

Dea had heard compliments like that for years. But for those words to come from him meant more to her than he would ever know.

"You look great out of uniform too."

Her daring comment caused him to laugh out loud before he closed the door and went around to get behind the wheel. She loved hearing his deep chuckle before he pulled onto the main road. The scent of the soap he used filled the interior. He drove with expertise, maneuvering through Rome's hectic evening traffic with ease.

To her surprise, they ended up at the heliport at the airport. She turned to him. "Where are we headed?"

"It's a surprise. We'll be at our destination within a half hour."

She took a deep breath. "That sounds exciting." Where on earth were they going?

"I hope it will be. Come on. The pilot is waiting for us."

Within minutes they'd climbed aboard the helicopter. She sat in the back while he took the copilot's seat. Dea was no stranger to flights in helicopters. Seeing Rome from the air was an experience she was very familiar with, but right now she couldn't focus on anything but the striking male seated in front of her.

The scenery changed and after a little while the helicopter dipped. She glimpsed Mount Vesuvius in the distance. Her breath quickened as they descended and suddenly the pilot set them down on a helipad. She looked out the windows and realized they'd landed on a *ship*.

Not just any ship.

He opened the door and put out his hand to help her down into the balmy night air. She turned to him in bewilderment. "You've brought us to the yacht."

Guido's jaw tightened perceptibly. Something was going on inside him she didn't understand. He drew her away from the helicopter. "Let's start again, Signorina Loti. Welcome to Naples."

Time stood still while Guido's words sank in. Dea's thoughts flew back to that night on the yacht when she'd been introduced to him. But in her mind, she hadn't been able to see him because his best friend had stood next to him and taken her breath.

"When you look back on that night, do you even remember me?" he asked in a teasing voice.

She swallowed hard. What did he want her to say? Dea needed help. "Rini turned and asked me to dance. I never had a chance to talk to you again."

"Would it surprise you if you knew *I'd* wanted to

be the one to dance with you first? But Rini stood closer to you."

Oh, no… "I had no idea. Your fath—"

"My father forced us on you and your model friend," he interrupted her. "But let's admit Rini was your choice. You couldn't take your eyes off him and I didn't stand a chance."

CHAPTER FOUR

DEA STARTED TO TREMBLE. She thought she'd put the memory of that night behind her, but Guido had brought it up because it had obviously been painful for him too. She'd heard it in his voice. "I—I'm sorry," she stammered.

"Don't be. It wasn't anyone's fault and it happened over a year ago. I brought you here in the hope that tonight I could wine and dine you with no other distractions."

He meant Rini.

This was the time for honesty no matter how frightened she was to discuss such a sensitive issue for both of them. "I admit I was attracted to Rini, but it was one-sided."

She heard him take a quick breath. "Are you over him?"

Guido knew how to go for the jugular. It was part of his makeup. She bit her lip. Rini was his best friend. The answer to Guido's loaded question could spell life or death for a future relationship with him. If he wanted one. She lifted her eyes to him.

"His looks filled an image I'd carried in my mind since I was a girl, but it had no substance. I was never into Rini, because he was a figment of my imagination. Amazingly, Alessandra carried that same image in her mind. We're not twins for nothing. But the moment she met Rini, that image took on substance for her and she fell hard.

"The beauty is, he fell hard for her too and pursued her. As you know, they're madly in love and terribly happy. Believe me when I tell you I'm beyond happy for them. I hope that answers your question. Please tell me it does," she pleaded with him.

After a long silence, he said, "Your honesty has blown me away." To her relief, he broke into a smile that melted her bones. "You're good at doing that."

"Am I never to hear the end of it?" she teased.

"I don't know. Come on." He cupped her elbow and walked her over to the covered dining area on the top deck. "Are you seeing another man right now, Dea?"

"No. What about you? Is there a woman in your life at the moment?"

"Only you."

One table had been set for them with candles and flowers. Guido helped her sit down, then poured some wine for both of them.

"I take it we're alone."

"I told you there'd be no distractions tonight."

The steward brought their food to the table and removed the covers. A wonderful aroma of fish with lemon and rosemary wafted in the night air.

She smiled. "In other words, your parents won't show up."

"Not tonight." His eyes searched hers. "Tell me—did they say or do something that made you uncomfortable at the wedding reception?"

"Not at all, Guido. I'm afraid I wasn't myself that day and am sorry if it showed."

But she could tell he wouldn't let it go when he asked, "Was it my father making you uncomfortable? What did he say when he talked to you and your friend after the fashion show?"

She put down her fork. "Nothing. He simply wanted us to meet you and your best friend before we left the yacht."

"Papà came on strong, didn't he?" Dea averted her eyes. "I knew it. There are times when he can be unbearable."

"That's because he loves you so much and is proud of you."

"You were probably afraid I was made in his image."

Guido was so intuitive it was scary. "You and your father bear a physical resemblance. Was he an outstanding soccer player too?"

"He had no interest in the sport."

"But he came to all your games."

"Yes."

"Lucky you."

"He's a hunter."

She took another bite of fish. "Do you hunt too?"

"Maybe once a year when I go with him, but I prefer fly-fishing. What about your father?"

Dea smiled. "Dad would rather camp out with our family."

"That's something else I'm crazy about," he informed her.

"It's so fun."

After the steward brought them a pastry dessert, Guido changed the subject. "What are you doing Saturday night?"

She got a fluttery feeling in her chest. "Gina and I are going to see *Othello*. We made arrangements for it last week."

"Then getting together with you this weekend is out since I have another match on Sunday in Bologna."

He'd be out of town. Maybe he was as disappointed as she was. "When will you be back?"

"Monday."

Dea wanted to see him again too. "What's your Monday evening like?"

A flicker lit up his eyes. "What do you have in mind?"

"After work I'll pick up some groceries and fix us dinner at my apartment."

"She cooks too?"

The warmth of his smile invaded her insides. "I spent years in the *castello* kitchen after school watching and learning from the cook. When she did her shopping in Metaponto on the weekends, I often went with her."

"But you don't have to cook for me."

"I'd like to. It's fun now that I can eat things I long for. The only drawback is cooking for one."

"I know what you mean. I normally eat out."

"So—" she rolled her eyes "—you chip, drop, kick, sweep and cook too?"

The corners of his arresting male mouth turned up. "Tell you what. After you get home from work on Monday, call me and I'll pick you up. We'll go shopping and spend a culinary evening together."

"Be sure to bring a video of your game against Bologna. I'd like to see at least a part of it."

"If we lose, I won't bother to bring it."

She studied him over the rim of her wineglass. "You *won't* lose."

"How do you know?" he whispered.

"Your team played its heart out last Sunday. I imagine they'll do it again and again."

"That's the kind of faith that helps me push them. On that positive note, I'll get us back to Rome."

"This was a long way to come, Guido. We could have gone anywhere to eat."

His features grew serious. "True. But it was important to me that I erase the bad memory of that night from my mind by doing this again."

She moaned inwardly. "I never meant t—"

"I know you didn't," he broke in. "We'll never talk about it again. Thank you for coming with me." He stood up and helped her from the table. They walked toward the helipad at the other end of the yacht with his arm at the back of her waist. The Bay of Naples glittered with lights, making a glorious sight. To be with Guido like this thrilled her.

"Please thank the steward and the cook. The food was delicious," she said before climbing in the helicopter.

"I'll tell them." She felt his hands squeeze her hips gently before she moved all the way inside. He shouldn't have touched her like that. It sent a voluptuous curl of heat through her body.

For Guido to bring her all the way here to clear up something so vital meant his attraction to her was more than skin-deep. Guido was a man of great substance. But he'd been hurt; otherwise he wouldn't have asked if she was over Rini. To embark on a relationship with him, they had to build total trust between them.

His sensitive nature had picked up on her pain at the wedding. If she got the chance, she'd explain to him that she'd been going through her own personal crisis that had nothing to do with his parents or anyone else.

Dea shivered. The whole issue with Rini was hard to explain, but it was long since over. Much as she was dying to get to know Guido better, she realized there were things he was holding back from her about himself. She would work on getting him to tell her what was wrong.

The flight from Bologna touched down at the airport at one on Monday afternoon. Their one–nil win had made the whole team giddy. After a training session at the stadium with the players and coaches, Guido drove home on fire for the evening planned with Dea.

It seemed like months instead of days since their dinner on Thursday night.

He watched the video of the game and made notes. But he kept waiting for the phone to ring and lost his concentration. When it finally rang and he saw the caller ID, he picked right up.

"Dea?"

"Are you back?"

"I've been at the apartment several hours. How are you?"

"Relieved to know you made it home safely." He liked hearing that. "Your win was all over the news last night. You must be ecstatic."

He was ecstatic all right, but she was the underlying reason for this joie de vivre he'd never felt before. "What time should I pick you up?"

"If you'll give me an hour, I'll be ready. But why don't we walk to the market at the Via della Pace? It's close and they'll have everything we need."

"I'll be outside the entrance waiting for you. *A presto*, Dea."

Guido showered and shaved. As he was finding out, anytime he was with Dea, surprising things happened. To go grocery shopping with her would no doubt be an adventure, followed by a casual night at home. It was exactly what he needed after the stressful weekend when once again he thought the team wouldn't win until the last few seconds.

He pulled on a sport shirt and jeans, grabbed the

disc with the video and left. Once he'd found a parking space near her apartment, he walked to the entrance expecting to have to wait. Instead she was outside drawing the interest of every male in the vicinity.

Why not? She was wearing taupe-colored trousers topped with a sheer flutter blouse in a pale blue. The hem fell to her waist, emphasizing the feminine curves of her body. A mesh shopping bag hung from her fingers.

Her long, sparkling brown hair with its gold highlights was tied at the nape with a thin pale blue ribbon. Her natural beauty staggered him. When she saw him, she broke into a smile that lit up her eyes. He moved closer, already feeling out of breath. "I've been looking forward to this evening."

"Me too. Are you hungry?"

She should know better than to ask him a question like that. "Starving. I skipped lunch in anticipation of tonight."

"Good. I plan to feed you well. We only need to buy a few items. It's just a short walk after we reach the corner."

"I want the exercise. It helps me unwind."

"I know what you mean."

Exhilarated to be with her, he headed down the street with her. "What's on the menu for tonight?"

"Chicken Tetrazzini. I thought it would be a nice change from fish."

"I like anything."

"Sounds like you're an easy man to please. Lucky

for me." They rounded the corner and soon arrived at the market. "Help me find chicken breasts, white mushrooms and linguine. I'll gather the rest."

"Like what?"

"Parmesan cheese, fresh garlic, onions, parsley and thyme, and cream."

"We'll need a good wine too."

"Why don't you pick it out."

He knew a Tuscan Chianti that would go well with their dinner. They worked together. She reached for some herb focaccia bread and he found a couple of *baba al limoncello* pastries.

Guido paid for the groceries and carried the bag home. It was bursting at the seams. He slanted her a glance. "Just a few items," he ribbed her.

"I guess I'm a typical woman after all. Sorry if it's heavier than a soccer ball…"

"I'm relieved your apartment is only a couple more steps away. I just might make it."

"Let's hope there's no reporter hanging around trying to take a picture of the famous soccer player in your sad condition." Her comments continually amused him. "Tell you what. Once we're inside, you can stretch out on the couch and watch the game while I cook."

"I thought *you* wanted to watch it."

"I do. I'll come in and out of the kitchen."

"That won't work. We'll cook together, then eat while we watch. I want to hear your commentary."

"It won't be worth much."

"Let me be the judge of that."

"The bathroom is down that hall if you'd like to freshen up."

"Thank you."

Her elegant apartment reminded him she was a woman who had the title of Princess Caracciolo and Taranto. But the way she behaved, you'd never know she came from a long line of aristocrats. She'd worked her way around the market picking out what she wanted and taking her time like any Italian house-wife. Surely he'd never seen a more beautiful one.

As he came out of the bathroom, he passed her bedroom, then backtracked in slow motion. On the wall next to the window was a poster. To his shock, it was the one of a younger Guido. She'd kept this one for herself. The sight of it gave him a heart attack.

He checked his breathing before going back to the living room. Within a half hour delicious aromas filled the apartment. She made a place on her coffee table in front of the television. He poured the wine while she went back to the kitchen for their plates.

Guido could see doing this for the rest of his life. Never had he been with a woman who caused his thoughts to expand as far as marriage. Since he'd taken her to the yacht, part of him was alarmed by the depth of his feelings for her because he didn't know if he trusted everything she'd told him concerning Rini.

He had no doubt she'd spoken the truth as much as she could admit. But he sensed there was more she was holding back from him. Since it involved his best friend, he couldn't be satisfied with a half confession any more than he could a half loaf of bread, especially not now, when he knew what was hanging on the wall in her bedroom. The poster's presence had to mean something vital.

He would have to go on seeing her to learn the whole truth. Maybe that would involve digging it out of her soul. Until then he would spend as much time as possible with her because he couldn't help himself. At this point she was on his mind day and night.

They watched part of the game, but she fired questions at him that suggested she really wanted to understand. He was only too happy to oblige.

"Are your players trained into the ground?"

His lips twitched. "Maybe not into the ground. On an individual basis they train by working out hard, running a lot, eating right, practicing skills. If you have a love for it, it isn't so hard."

She sat back against the cushion of the couch. "So what part do you play as the owner?"

"I'm like one of the coaches and get right in there. When we're not out on the field, the players work out in the gym. I work on them to focus on abs and quads. They need to increase their agility and endurance."

A glint of amusement entered her marvelous eyes. "Do they hate to see you coming?"

"Always. When the other coaches are through, I usually make the team run a variety of drills and practice plays. I force them to concentrate on being as fit as possible by combining sprints with long runs."

"Well, it's certainly paying off. You've only lost one game this year."

"True, but we barely won yesterday's. That's got me nervous. I don't want the team to get comfortable."

She took another sip of wine. "Do you have a motto?"

He nodded. "Discipline yourself so others don't!"

"What a great slogan! It makes perfect sense."

"I'm glad you approve."

"Are you kidding? Let's watch the end of the game and see if your team has taken your words to heart."

After fifteen minutes it was over. She wanted to know how many players were on a team, their positions and tactical skills. "How did you train when you were high school age?"

"I started soccer at seven."

"I should have remembered that."

Even if she was being polite, it flattered him that she would show this much interest in the game.

"During the summers, when I had no guidance, I'd start by running hills with my friends. Later on I'd work on sprints and sudden bursts of speed. Then again, I always had to have a ball at my feet so I wouldn't lose touch until soccer practice started.

"I went to as many matches as I could attend and played every position, including defender, goalie and midfield. But my favorite position was forward."

"The position you excelled at until you became the epic champion."

His brows lifted. "Epic?"

"That's you. I'm truly in awe of you, Guido."

"It's past history."

"But that excellence is living on in your team. Are you happy you left the shipping company to do this?"

"Yes, but whether I decide to own and manage a soccer team for the rest of my life isn't a question I can answer yet."

"I bet your father wants you back."

"Yes, but I won't do it unless I can embrace it a hundred percent. Let me ask you a question. Are you happy your modeling career is behind you?"

A shadow entered her eyes. "You want to know the truth?"

"What do you think?"

"I went to college to study fashion design, something I'd always been interested in. But by the time I was halfway through, I couldn't seem to produce something that wasn't mediocre. I felt like Salieri in the film *Amadeus*."

Guido would have laughed if he didn't know how serious this was. "You're referring to the Italian composer at the time of Mozart."

"Yes. As someone put it, you have to squint your ears and listen for the magic. If you can sense a supernatural beauty within, you know it's Mozart. If it's just music, it's not Mozart and probably someone like Salieri."

"You were awfully hard on yourself."

"I know. Halfway through school I was approached by the agency that hired me to model for them. I thought I'd take a year off school and try it."

Guido was fascinated. "Did you love it?"

"*Love* is a strong word. I enjoyed the first year

very much, but after that I sensed a lot was lacking in my life. The problem was, I felt it was too soon to give it up. I knew I could go back to school, but what if I failed to find my true calling? The owners of the agency put a lot of pressure on me to remain with them."

"You made a lot of money for them."

"Money runs the world." She didn't sound happy about it. For once he'd met a woman who wasn't impressed by the Rossano name and fortune.

"So tell me how you came to work for Juliana Parma now."

She shook her head. "I don't want to bore you."

"You mean the way I've bored you for the last two hours?"

A small laugh escaped her throat. She looked at him. "Throughout my life, my parents and aunt and uncle have taken me to the opera. I'd sit in my seat and envy the singers whose voices could bring such pleasure to people, to me. I cried through every opera. I thought if God had given me a great voice, I would go on singing forever."

His throat thickened with emotion. "God gave you another gift, Dea. You've thrilled a lot of people modeling the clothes of famous fashion designers."

She sat forward. "That's the point. It was the designers who created all the haute couture fashions. I envied their brilliance. All I did was walk around to display them."

"But those designers needed a woman like you to carry them off to the greatest advantage."

"Thank you for trying to build me up. In time I realized that the only thing that could make me truly happy was to create something of my own, something that came from me. That's probably how you feel about soccer. It comes from *you*, no one else."

Dea got that right. "When I saw you and Alessandra in that video, even at your young age your father acknowledged that you had an aptitude for design."

"That's because I wasn't good at anything else."

"I could argue with you, but I'm afraid you wouldn't listen. Go on and tell me about Juliana."

"Many times our family went backstage to talk to her. I saw how much she loved her work and I could understand because her creations brought life to the singers on the stage. The richness of the sets and clothes makes the opera so fantastic.

"When you watch them perform in street clothes, it's so different from casting them into their parts with all the trappings. It's a kind of magic she creates.

"After I went back to finish school, I knew I wanted to do what she did." Tears filled her eyes. "My aunt made it possible for me to work under her this semester. You'll never know what a great honor that is."

"I think I do. I've attended many operas in my life. What you've admitted helps me understand why I've enjoyed it so much."

"She designs for the theater too. The other night Gina and I were engrossed in the costuming for *Othello*. Bringing in the Moorish elements made it very exciting. In the future I hope I can be a part of such a project."

"With a drive like yours, I have no doubts." It was getting late and he knew she had work early in the morning. The last thing he wanted to do was overstay his welcome, but he needed to do this right. He sensed in his gut this woman could change his life. "Let me help with the dishes before I leave."

"Those are my department tonight."

"Your food was fabulous. I hope you know that."

"Thank you." He reached for the disc and she walked him to the door. "I'm so glad you came over tonight."

"We'll have to do it again. I'll be in touch."

She opened the door. "I'd like that."

Much as he wanted to crush her in his arms and kiss the daylights out of her, he didn't dare. He was a greedy man. The poster on her wall still wasn't enough. He wanted to hear her bare her soul to him.

Like Carla, who'd hovered in the recesses of his mind because she'd judged him lacking, was Rini still lurking somewhere in her psyche because he hadn't wanted her? That's what he needed to find out. But that kind of deeply buried secret would take time to emerge—he'd have to get the whole truth from her. He couldn't be with her much longer and not find out.

"Thank you for tonight." He cupped the side of her lovely face with his hand before walking down the hall to the elevator. The warmth of her skin stayed with him all the way out to his car for the drive home.

CHAPTER FIVE

THURSDAY EVENING AT the close of work, Gina and her fiancé, Aldo, were waiting for Dea at the front entrance. After introductions were made, the cute auburn-haired mechanic shook her hand.

"Thanks for the poster. Since you won't take any money for it, let us buy you dinner."

"That's very nice of you, but I have a better idea. How would you like to see the soccer game on Sunday?"

"I can only afford seats behind the goalie."

"I know a better place to sit and have a friend who'll lower the price for you."

He squinted at her. "Are you serious?"

"Yes. Follow me to the stadium and we'll buy them now. You can tour the museum at the same time. It doesn't close until seven." Now Dea had a great excuse to see the videos of Guido without his thinking she was chasing after him.

"That would be wonderful!" Gina hugged her.

"I must be dreaming," Aldo murmured. "I've heard this game is already a sellout."

"One thing I've learned—they always have tickets. I'll get my car."

She hurried off. Before long the three of them arrived at the stadium and parked near the suite of offices. There was a long line of people waiting to buy tickets. "Why don't you get in line while I go in the museum. I'll only be a minute."

When she went inside, she saw that another man was in charge. She went up to him. "Is there any way I can talk to Sergio if he's here?"

His eyes swept over her. "You're the famous model!"

"Past tense. Could you get in touch with him?"

"He's running the ticket booth. Maybe I can help."

"Thank you, but no. He's the one I have to talk to."

"Just a minute." He pulled out his phone and made a call. After a minute Sergio walked in the rear door. She ran over to him.

"I'm sorry to bother you, but I need a favor. There's a couple at the back of the ticket line. He has dark red hair. Give him the very best seats you can for Sunday's game, but only charge him the cheapest price. I'll make up the rest." She opened her wallet and pulled out enough euros to cover it.

"I'll be happy to. Don't go away."

"I won't. After they get the tickets, we're going to spend time in here. Maybe you can give him the royal tour. It would mean everything to him and a lot to me."

"Sure thing."

He left through the same door. Dea thanked the other man and went outside to find Gina. Fifteen minutes later they'd bought their tickets. It wasn't until they headed for the museum that Aldo cried, "Do you know who that guy was who sold me the tickets? Sergio Colombo! He's only the greatest soccer player in Italy next to Guido Rossano. And these are the best seats in the stadium!"

Gina flashed Dea a smile of such gratitude it warmed her clear through.

"Now that you're set, let's take a tour before it closes."

Some moments in life were precious. Sergio gave them a personalized visit with anecdotes about Guido she'd never forget. The videos thrilled her to the core. When they thanked him and turned to leave, the man who stole her breath every time she saw him stood in the doorway.

"Guido…"

He moved toward her. "Why don't you introduce me to your friends."

Sergio must have told him she was here. If he'd still been in his office, then he'd had to come only a few steps. Before she could say a word, Aldo walked toward them. "I can't believe it. Guido Rossano. I've idolized you for years. Gina—" he drew her along "—this is the legend."

"It's an honor to meet you at last." She shook his hand. "Thanks to Dea, this day has come."

"Have you been well taken care of?" No one could be more charming or dashing than Guido.

Aldo beamed. "This is about the best day of my life!"

Dea was touched to see a grown man so happy to meet a boyhood idol.

"They'll be at the match on Sunday," Dea informed him.

"Why don't you two pick a poster before you leave and I'll sign it."

"You mean it?" Aldo's eyes widened. "How about the one at the national championship."

Sergio pulled it out of the bin and put it on the counter. He handed Guido a felt-tip pen. Gina looked at Sergio. "We'd like a signed poster of you too. I'll pay for it."

"No, no. It's on the house."

A minute later Dea saw two people ready to leave the store looking like they'd been given all their Christmases at once. She turned to the first man running the museum, then Sergio and Guido. "Thank you all." But as she started to follow her friends out the door, Guido said, "Where do you think you're going?"

Dea looked around. "Home."

"Do you have to drive them?"

"No. We came in our own cars."

"Good. That saves me a trip. Come to my office with me first."

"All right." After taking a breath, she turned and called to Gina, "I'll see you tomorrow." They waved back.

To her surprise, Guido put an arm around her shoulders in front of the other men and swept her through the back doorway, a shortcut to his inner sanctum. "I don't want the guys thinking they have a chance with you."

She blushed. "They were both so nice."

He took her inside his office and shut the door. "If you want to know the truth, it's not every day the ravishing Dea makes an appearance at a soccer stadium not once, but twice. One more time and their hearts might not be able to take it."

"You idiot." She pushed against his chest playfully and was rewarded by being crushed against him.

His eyes pierced hers. "You really don't have any idea what you do to a man, do you? I'm going to kiss you so you'll find out." Guido's intensity shook her before his head descended and his mouth closed over hers. Enveloped in heat, she felt his hands roam over her back and hips, urging her closer so she could feel every hard muscle and sinew in his body.

Though Dea had been with a few men who'd wanted to kiss her passionately, she hadn't fully reciprocated. Something had always held her back... until now.

This was different. Guido was different.

The feel of his mouth slowly devouring hers created such divine sensations that she felt like she'd been born for this moment and couldn't get enough. "Guido," she gasped in pleasure as he drew her into a wine-dark rapture. She clung to him, and they moved and breathed like they were a part of each other. Emotions greater than she could describe took over now that Guido had swept her into his arms.

She was already crazy about the man, but the sheer

physical feeling at this moment was all consuming, burning everything in its path so there was no room for anything else. Mind, body and soul were on fire for one man who answered the question of her existence.

"My office is no place for this. Come home with me, Dea," he whispered against her lips, swollen from the refined savagery of his kisses. "I need to be with you more than you can imagine," he confessed in a ragged voice.

I want that too, Guido. I'm in love with you. I know I am. But if you only need me, and aren't in love with me, then I can't let this go any further.

After one more long, hungry kiss, he opened the door. She was so dazed she would have fallen if he hadn't helped her to her car.

"I—I don't think I can drive." Her voice faltered.

"Let me. My car is in the private parking area. I'll come back for it tomorrow."

She shook her head. No matter how much she wanted to go home with him and throw away the key, she didn't plan to spend the night with him. "You mustn't leave yours here. I'll follow you."

Guido kept Dea in his sights for the short drive to his apartment. Once she'd pulled alongside him in his private parking garage, they took the elevator to the second floor. It wasn't until they'd entered his apartment that he realized he'd never brought a woman here before.

He turned on the lights. "Forgive my generic apartment that has no personality."

"Oh, yes, it does. You can tell in an instant that a bachelor lives here."

He flicked her an amused glance. "That bad, huh?"

Her eyes smiled. "It tells me you're a practical man. No nonsense about you. You certainly don't have to make excuses to me."

"Nevertheless, I want to explain that the convenience of the location to the stadium makes it ideal, and it serves as my base for eating and sleeping while I'm living in Rome."

"Where did you live before?"

"Naples. But I sold that apartment when I moved here. It would have been pointless to keep it. I'm afraid it didn't have any personality, either." She laughed quietly.

Guido studied her features. "Is that what you really think about me? No nonsense?"

One brow lifted. "When you were teaching me some soccer moves behind the castle, you were all business. But on second thought, maybe the Lamborghini doesn't quite match the profile of the down-and-out bachelor who doesn't need more than a roof over his head."

"Do you know something, Dea Caracciolo? I've never laughed as much with anyone else."

"You should do it more often. It's very attractive."

His pulse raced. If he got started on Dea's attributes, he'd never stop. After those moments in his office he still hadn't recovered from being set on fire. His desire for her was off the charts.

If she was worried he was about to carry her straight to the bedroom, she ought to be. He'd already broken his own rule about not rushing things with her. He hadn't been able to help it. *Slow down, Rossano.* "Have you had dinner?"

"Not yet. Gina and Aldo surprised me as I was leaving work this evening. They wanted to take me for a meal to thank me for the poster. I told him to save his money for soccer tickets and we went straight to the stadium. You and your staff were so nice to them."

"It was our pleasure." Holding on to his last vestige of self-control, he said, "The restroom is down that hall if you'd like to freshen up first."

"I'd love it. Thank you."

"I'll be in the kitchen. I know I saw eggs and cheese in there this morning and will whip something up for us."

"Perfect."

Guido headed there and made tasty omelets they ate at the kitchen table. He produced some oranges to go with their meal.

"Hmm. These are gorgeous." He watched her finish the last section of her fruit and thought he'd never seen or tasted such a luscious mouth. "So were the eggs. You're a terrific cook."

"Thank you."

"Having lived on your own for so long, you're probably a great chef and don't know it."

He chuckled. "What I am is a nervous wreck now that the soccer season is coming to an end. Three more games now that it's May."

"How many at home?"

"One. The others will be in Cagliari and Siena."

She sat back in the chair drinking her coffee. "Has owning this team been fulfilling for you? Can you see doing this for years and years?"

Her interest sounded genuine. If he had his heart's desire, he could see doing just about anything. "I don't know. My father's not getting any younger. His emotional pull on me to come back to the shipping lines is strong."

"You're his only son. That puts you in a vulnerable position."

He nodded. "But Papà has two brothers and they have three sons who also sit on the board. And there's my grandfather. At ninety-five, he still wields influence with my father."

She cocked her head. "I understand from Alessandra that you're the light of your grandfather's life. He believes you're the one in the family to take Rossano Shipping Lines in a new direction."

"But that's my father's decision, no one else's." Guido swallowed the rest of his coffee. Here they were talking in his kitchen instead of picking up where they'd left off in his office. He feared she was thankful for the breathing room between them effectively lowering the heat.

"If you're through eating, let's go in the living

room. I want to talk to you about something important."

Those fabulous orbs narrowed. "I thought that's what we're doing."

Until he learned everything hiding inside her, he knew he would never have peace. "It's more comfortable in there."

She averted her eyes, a subtle sign of nervousness. "First I'll just clear our dishes."

"Not tonight. Remember your rule? It applies at my house in reverse. After you."

Resigned to do Guido's bidding, Dea went through to the living room and sat on one of the chairs near the couch. He'd followed her, but the tension radiating from him let her know something was wrong. "What is it?"

In a surprise move Guido leaned over her and put his hands on the arms of the chair, virtually trapping her. With his lips so close to hers, she couldn't think, let alone breathe.

"We entered deeper waters this evening. Though I want to carry you to my bedroom and make love to you all night, we need to talk before we can no longer feel the sand beneath our feet. I won't be able to go on seeing you until I have all the honesty in you," his voice rasped.

All her honesty? "What do you mean?"

"If you're holding anything back where your feelings for Rini are concerned, I need to know."

After those words he gave her a long, lingering

kiss that left her trembling before he released her and sat on the couch across from her with his hands clasped between his legs.

His eyes had taken on a haunted look, as if he couldn't make up his mind about her. Sickness swept through her.

"I've told you everything! I don't know why you don't believe me. I think what you meant to say is, you need to hear all the dishonesty in me. The problem is, I'm not sure I *could* identify all of it and agree that to go on seeing each other would be a waste of time."

Either Rini or Alessandra had betrayed her and told Guido every ugly detail about her past. One of them had undoubtedly gone so far as to reveal the details of that tumultuous period in the past when Alessandra's boyfriend had betrayed her and chased after Dea. No other explanation would explain why the earth had suddenly tilted.

Now that Guido knew her history, it didn't surprise her that he wanted to understand her behavior from her own lips. If he was hoping it was all a lie, Dea couldn't help him out.

She'd thought she'd put all the misery behind her and was endeavoring to become a better person who had faith in herself. But there'd be no convincing Guido of anything. The damage was too great for her to fight for him.

What a fool she'd been to let her guard down. Now she'd fallen in love with him, and she knew this was the one fatal mistake in life she'd never recover from.

There was no one like Guido, but he was beyond reach.

On unsteady legs she got to her feet and reached for her purse on the coffee table. "There's nothing more for me to say. Goodbye, Guido."

Before Dea broke down and dissolved into tears, she left the apartment and hurried to the parking garage for her car. She could hear him call out to her, but she didn't stop. When she backed around, he stood in her way looking fierce and so handsome it hurt.

"You're not going anywhere."

Her breath caught. "You worded that wrong. *We're* not going anywhere. All the family secrets are out. It could never work for you and me. Please move aside. It's late and I have to be up early in the morning."

In the dim light of the garage his face seemed to have lost color. "I can't let you go until we talk this out. You've obviously misunderstood me."

"No, I haven't," she fired back. "You were crystal clear."

Her words rang in the air. He finally stepped aside so she could drive out to the street. Her last glimpse of him through the mirror reflected a man wearing a mask so bleak she hardly recognized him.

Dea drove to her own apartment. When she walked inside, she was aware that the recent joy she'd been experiencing had left her soul. Before going to bed, she removed the poster of Guido from the wall. Unable to throw it away yet, she rolled it up and put it in the closet.

Once under the covers, she buried her face in the

pillow until it was wet. *No prince is going to find you, Dea.* From here on out it was work and more work to get through this life.

Friday morning after sleeping poorly, she got dressed, skipped breakfast and worked out in the gym. One of the guys on duty there, who was a big flirt, came over to bother her. He couldn't be a day over twenty-four.

"When are you going to let me take you out?"

"Never."

"Ooh. That was brutal."

Dea was in a brutal mood. Even if it was her fault, her experiences with men had brought her nothing but misery. "I can see three women in here at least five years younger than I am. I'm sure they'd love your attention."

"They're not you."

"Lucky them."

Her comment got rid of him for the moment. She took advantage of the time to slip back out and grab a cappuccino on her way to the shop. Today they were having a meeting to discuss a few of the men's costumes for *Don Giovanni.*

She welcomed the busy day so she wouldn't give in to her agony over losing Guido.

There was no one she could confide in about this, not even her aunt. It saddened her because she'd been getting along with her whole family for a long time. The next time her mom let her know Rini and Alessandra had gone back to Positano for a while, she'd fly home to visit her parents. Her parents could always fly here. That was the only way to avoid more pain.

At quitting time Gina came over to her table, her face beaming. "I'll never be able to thank you enough for what you've done. Aldo's a different person. Are you going to be at the game on Sunday with Guido?"

"I plan to," she lied without compunction. She didn't want to talk about him, not ever again. While their heads were together, the receptionist came in the room and approached her.

"Some flowers arrived for you, Dea. At first I thought they must be for Juliana until I saw the card with your name. They're out in the reception room on my desk." Her brows lifted. "Three dozen red roses! Someone's in love."

Dea's heart did a double kick. "I'll be out in a minute. Thank you."

Gina nudged her. "Guido Rossano is absolutely crazy about you. If I didn't like you so much, I'd be horribly envious."

"You've got Aldo."

"Yeah. I do, but there's no one quite like the *Cuor di Leone*."

Her eyes closed. Gina was right. Guido was unique in so many ways she could hardly breathe just thinking about him. Why did he bother to send her anything? He could have no idea how painful this was for her.

"Well, come on," Gina urged her. "It's time to go home. If you're not dying to look at them, I am."

Dea took a quick breath. "Okay." She grabbed her purse and followed her friend. The second they reached the foyer, the heavy perfume from the roses assailed her. They both gasped as she walked over to the enormous spray and reached for the card perched in a little plastic pick. *You have to forgive me. I said everything wrong and want to start over.*

Tears stung her eyelids. She pressed the card to her heart. They couldn't start over.

Gina stood behind her. "If you'll bring your car around, I'll help you put these flowers in the backseat so you can take them home."

Before the flowers could be placed inside the car, Dea and Gina had to tip the vase to pour out the water. Somehow they managed. "Thank you," she said to her friend before driving home.

After parking in her space, Dea had some difficulty taking the roses out of the car so the heads wouldn't get broken off.

"Let me help," sounded a deep, familiar male voice behind her.

She started to tremble. "Guido—"

"I've waited here wondering if you'd bring them home or throw them away at work. I have my answer."

Dea should have tossed them. Now she'd been caught in the act.

"I'll bring them in. You go ahead and open the door for me."

Guido had left her no choice. When they reached her apartment, he carried them out to the kitchen to fill the vase with water. He darted her a glance. "I meant what I said on the card. I need to start over with you by taking you for a drive in the country.

We'll stop at some spot for dinner and talk. Please don't deny me this."

"You already know everything there is to know about me. There's no need for more talk."

"We haven't even started," he came back. His dark blue eyes glittered. "Let's get something straight. We may have been the closest of friends all our lives, but I swear before God that Rini has *never* discussed you with me. Neither has Alessandra, so you can put that misconception out of your head once and for all."

Was he speaking the truth? Dea wanted to believe him.

No matter how hard she fought it, the force of his words and personality cut through her defenses like a sharp knife. Not only that, he was wearing a dusky blue jacket over a cream shirt open at the throat and beige trousers. His masculine beauty melted her on the spot. It wasn't fair. She could feel herself weakening.

"I—I need to shower first," she stammered.

"While you do that, I'll carry these roses into the living room and put them on the coffee table. I want you to see my apology every time you enter your apartment."

Oh, Guido…

Dea hurried to her room and got ready. She chose a dressy peach blouse and skirt. After brushing out her hair and leaving it loose, she joined him in the living room. The red roses had already filled it with their fragrance.

She was probably a fool to go with him, but she'd

promised herself not to make snap judgments any-more. Tonight she would hear him out one last time, but this was it.

Quiet reigned as Guido drove them a short distance from Rome to Lake Nemi, which was set in the cra-ter of an ancient volcano. He turned on some music. Neither of them felt the need to talk. That suited Dea, who was waiting for an explanation from him when he was ready.

She sat back to enjoy the landscape, especially since she'd never been here before. The lush nature preserve surrounding the lake came as a pleasant sur-prise. He took them to a charming restaurant border-ing the water and asked for them to be seated in an isolated area. The waiter led them to a candlelit table for two separated by ornamental trees.

Guido ordered their meal. Wine and *cacio e pepe*, a dish of Pecorino Romano cheese and pasta to die for. Halfway through their meal she eyed him frankly. "This is delicious. The flowers were lovely too, but I'm still waiting for you to tell me why you don't think I've been totally honest with you. That hurt, you know? More than you can imagine."

He leaned forward. "I believe you've told me the truth, but—"

"But what?" she cried softly.

"Maybe you're still in denial over deep feelings you don't realize are there?"

"I take it you're talking about Rini, the prover-bial elephant in the room." His sustained silence con-firmed her suspicions. "You're still afraid I'm in love with my brother-in-law, and you want chapter and verse, is that it?" She put her napkin on the table. "Sorry I can't change history to make it more palatable for you, Guido."

His brows furrowed. "I'm not asking for that," he insisted.

"No? It sounds to me like you're asking for blood, so now you're going to get it. Long before that night, I'd been floundering emotionally when it came to men. Since childhood the image of the perfect man had lived in my imagination, but no man ever thrilled me to the point that I wanted to marry him."

"Until Rini," he grated.

"Yes. I took one look at him and no one else existed for me. The fact that there was no substance to back up that feeling—only a girl's dream—didn't stop me from throwing myself at him. When I say *throw*, I mean I slid my hands up his chest and kissed him with hunger. I'd never done such a thing in my life and assumed he had to feel the same way, but he didn't kiss me back. In truth, he couldn't get rid of me fast enough."

Even with his tan, Guido's complexion had gone ashen. "Stop, Dea—"

"No! I haven't finished. You wanted the unvarnished truth? Well, here it is. I suggested we get together the next evening, but he said he wouldn't be in town. After thanking me for the dance, he walked away without saying anything about seeing me again. I left the yacht in shock."

Guido's grim expression couldn't prevent her from

getting everything off her chest. "He was the second man in my life to do real damage."

"What do you mean, the second?"

"Rini didn't share that with you?"

"I told you. You were never a topic of conversation between us."

"I see. Well, years ago Alessandra's fiancé made a play for me and followed me to Rome. I never encouraged him. He swore he was in love with me, but the minute he got there, he went off with another model. The incident not only put me off taking any man seriously, but made me feel horrible for my sister and it drove a knife in her heart. Both of us had been so hurt it took us years to become friends again."

"You don't have to say another word." Clearly uncomfortable over the direction of the conversation, Guido got to his feet. After leaving some bills on the table, he walked around to her chair. "Come on. Let's go out to the car."

Still fired up, she walked quickly without letting him touch her. The second they got in the Lamborghini, she turned to him. "I know you don't like hearing this, but you wanted *all* of my truth."

"I never meant to cause you this kind of pain."

"Maybe not," she admitted, but Dea was too far gone now. At a glance, his profile resembled chiseled stone, but that didn't stop her from telling him everything.

"Simply put, Rini's rejection put me in the blackest hole of my life. Who could imagine a greater irony than the one where he met my sister and fell madly in love with her? They say lightning doesn't strike twice in the same place, but it did with me. I needed help. If it hadn't been for my family and my therapist, who pulled me out of that abyss, I don't know what would have happened."

"Please don't say any more."

"I have to. You wanted an answer. After many talks I began to figure out my life. Alessandra and I are now closer than we ever were throughout our childhood and have come to a perfect understanding.

"She knows that Rini represented the figment of my imagination that had lived inside me for years. He didn't know me from Adam and had no interest in me. So for me to feel rejected by him tells you the precarious state of my mental health."

Traffic was light entering Rome. It didn't take long to reach her apartment and drive to her parking level on the third floor.

"In time I worked through my humiliation. Rini was very kind and told me to forget it. Whatever he chose to tell Alessandra is their business, but she knows the whole truth. At her wedding I realized any amorous feelings for him had been wiped clean from my heart. Soon after that I gave up modeling and went back to college."

Without saying anything, Guido turned off the car and reached for the door handle. She told him not to bother. "I don't want you to see me inside my apartment. In fact I don't want to see you again. You have a trust issue with me that will never go away. I understand where you're coming from, but I can't be with a man who won't ever be free of his suspicions. Something, someone, has robbed you of your ability to trust."

Dea let herself out of the car. Before she shut the door, she said, "Let me leave you with this thought, which you can choose to believe or not. If you or your parents felt slighted by me at the reception, it wasn't intentional. What you sensed was my shame because you were his best friend and had witnessed my brazen behavior that night on the yacht.

"No one could expect you to forget that. But please be assured of one thing. I've loved getting to know the former *Cuor di Leone*."

"Dea—"

"*Adio per sempre*, Guido."

"Goodbye forever?" he ground out.

"Just what I said." She shut the door. Wild with pain, she hurried toward the entrance leading to her apartment.

CHAPTER SIX

"YOU'RE NOT RUNNING away from me again." Guido caught up to Dea and wrapped his strong arms around her from behind so she was trapped. His breathing was as ragged as hers. "I'm not letting you go until you agree to spend all day tomorrow with me."

She moved her head from side to side. "There's no point."

"Of course there is! You're right about me. I do have trust issues and need you. I want to show you the real me. I know in my gut you and I are good for each other. Give me tomorrow to turn this around, Dea. You can't mean things to end this way. I couldn't take it." He held her tighter, sounding frantic.

Once again she could feel herself giving in to him. "You have a game this weekend."

"On Sunday. Tomorrow is Saturday. I'll be here in the morning at seven thirty. Where we're going, it will be sunny and you'll want to wear something casual. We'll be gone the whole day and won't be home until late. Promise me you'll be ready when I come for you."

His body was actually trembling like hers. Feeling the strength of his emotions made it impossible to deny him. "I…promise."

"Grazie a Dio."

"Buonanotte, Guido." Before he tried to kiss her, she reached for the door handle and hurried inside the building.

Once in her apartment, Dea dashed to her bedroom and pulled out her cell phone. There was only one person she could talk to about how she was feeling. She needed her twin. The two of them had suffered through so much. Alessandra, now a married woman with a child, would understand Dea's pain and fear as no one else could.

Her sister answered on the third ring. "Dea?"

"I know it's late, but I need some advice. If Rini is right there, maybe you could call me back later?"

"No, no. I'm back in Positano. He's still with our parents working, but will be home tomorrow."

Dea was glad she hadn't disturbed them. "How's Brazzo?"

"Thriving. I put him to bed several hours ago."

"Then you don't mind if we talk?"

"Are you kidding? I've been dying to know if you've seen or heard from Guido since that weekend when we were all together. But in case nothing came of it, I was afraid to ask any questions."

Her eyes closed tightly. "Quite a lot has gone on, actually."

"Oh, Dea—that's the best news!" She heard pure happiness in her sister's voice. "I just love Guido. He's a fantastic man. You two seemed so great together I couldn't believe it. Rini thought the same thing. To quote him, you were 'like two halves of the same incredible whole.'"

It had felt that way to Dea. "We've been out several times. He's been by Juliana's office and sent me roses. Tomorrow we're spending a whole day together."

"Meraviglioso!"

"I don't know, Alessandra. That's why I'm calling."

"What's wrong?"

"He's been relentless in getting me to bare my soul to him. Now that I have, he—he's afraid I'll always have feelings for Rini," she stammered. "I don't know what more I can say or do to convince him otherwise."

"From what Rini has told me, Guido has always been as closed up as my husband when it comes to the personal. He's a deep one."

Dea shivered. "I've already learned that about him. I'm frightened to spend any more time with him."

"Because you feel doomed to love a man who isn't sure of you, right?"

"Exactly." Dea knew her sister would understand. "I can't think of anything worse than having to prove myself to him over and over."

"I can think of one thing."

"What's that?"

"Never seeing him again."

She gripped the phone tighter. "You're right. The thought of his being gone out of my life is anathema to me."

"He's exciting, all right. Something must have hap-

pened over the years that has made him so distrust-
ful. If you want my advice, do to him what he did to
you. Stick to him like glue until you uncover *his* secrets. When that day comes, he'll get the point that
he's the only male in your universe."

Was that possible?

"Thanks for talking to me, Alessandra. I'll do what
you said, but I'm so nervous."

"So was I when I flew to Positano to surprise Rini
long before we were married. It was a bad time for us
and I was terrified he'd tell me to go home and never
darken his doorstep again."

"You knew he wouldn't say that to you."

"No. Not then I didn't. There's no man more for-
bidding than Rini when he's upset. All I can say is,
I'm thrilled to hear Guido hasn't left you alone. Just
keep doing the unexpected."

"We'll see." But it took courage she didn't have
a lot of. "Give the baby hugs for me until I can see
him again."

"I will. And when you're with Guido tomorrow,
tell him Brazzo adores the purple octopus. Between
the color and the bells, I'm positive it's his favorite
toy."

"I'll relay the message. I'm sure it will please him."

"Dea? Do me one more favor. Keep me informed.
I'll be dying until I hear from you again."

"I promise. Love you."

"Love you too."

She clicked off. It was hard to believe that after

so many years of pain, the two of them were close again in a brand-new way.

At seven twenty in the morning Guido parked his car in front of Dea's apartment building and hurried inside to ring her on the foyer phone.

"There's no need for you to come up, Guido. I'll be right down and meet you at the car."

Elated that she was ready, he went back outside to wait for her. Though it was semicloudy in Rome, there'd be full sunshine where they were going.

Every time he saw her, she wore something different. Five foot seven and beautifully built, she could wear anything and look fabulous. This morning she'd put on white jeans with cuffs at the ankles and strappy beige sandals. On top she wore a round-necked three-quarter-sleeve cotton sweater in a soft hyacinth color. She left her freshly washed hair loose. It sparkled in the light. Best not to eat her up until they were alone.

"Buongiorno, bellissima." He opened the car door and helped her inside before going around to get behind the wheel. "I hope you haven't had breakfast yet."

"Just coffee."

"Good. We'll eat on the plane." He pulled into the traffic and headed for the airport.

She glanced at him from eyes the color of vintage Burgundy. "Are we flying to Naples again?"

"Si, signorina. But we won't be visiting the yacht."

"Are you going to take me on a sightseeing tour of your childhood haunts?" The question intrigued him.

"Would you like that?"

"I'd love to see the places that helped shape you into the person you are."

"We'll do that another day. Today I don't want to think about the past."

Her brows furrowed. "Why would you say that? Is it so painful?"

"That was an interesting choice of words."

"But the right one obviously. Otherwise you wouldn't question my asking."

He was glad they'd reached the airport so he could avoid an answer until they were on board the plane eating breakfast.

"Before we land in Naples, I'll try to explain myself. I grew up an only child. Since you were a twin, you can't possibly comprehend what it was like for me. My parents couldn't have more children and my father refused to adopt. He wanted a child from his blood. My mother was eager for more children, but it didn't happen."

"I'm sorry for all your sakes."

"My parents' marriage suffered because of my father's refusal to make my mother happy. His intransigence broke her heart. Ever since he said no to the idea of adoption, Papà has been paying for the damage he did to their union."

"So you became the golden child who had to meet your father's every expectation."

Guido nodded. "From the time I could comprehend pressure, I felt like I had to be perfect in his eyes to make him happy. I knew he expected me to follow in his footsteps. But I loved playing soccer and saw the disappointment in his eyes when I had to leave for practice or another game. He warned me that a life of sports wouldn't give me stability."

"That couldn't have been pleasant for you."

"No, but what made it worse was the fact that he was right."

"What do you mean?"

"In my late teens I had a serious girlfriend named Carla."

"You did?" At last he was revealing something vital about himself.

"I imagined us getting married one day after I'd had my run at soccer. But after I gave it up to go back to work for my father, she went off with another soccer player. When I realized it was the celebrity status of being the wife of a high-profile athlete she wanted, not me, I became wary of women."

Her eyes looked wounded as they played over him. "I'm sure that hurt a great deal."

"It made me angry. I did go back to work for my father, but I wasn't happy. The rest you know. Last year I left the company to buy a minor team. Not only have I turned out to be a great disappointment to Papà by leaving the business for a time, I'm a thirty-two-year-old bachelor.

"For the last five years he's been pushing me to get married. I know what's motivating his overzealous methods of throwing women at me. He wants me to provide grandchildren, hoping it will ease my mother's pain."

"So *that* was why he allowed the fashion show to take place on board the yacht."

"Of course. He planned it to coincide with my birthday because he wanted us to meet. Since nothing else had worked over the years, why not introduce me to the supermodel who's been the talk of Italy? With his reasoning, no real man could resist you, certainly not his own son.

"For once in his life, my father was right. Rini and I had been talking when Papà brought you and your friend over to your table. I'd seen your pictures everywhere, but meeting you in the flesh was something else."

Dea moaned. "When you and I were at the wedding reception, I was afraid I'd offended you when I made the remark about my friends hoping to do another fashion show on the yacht."

"I think you know by now that didn't offend me."

She nodded. "I'm afraid I've jumped to too many conclusions."

"So have I. I don't know how much you know about Rini and me. We met at seven years of age and attended the same schools together until college. The two of us went through every good and bad time together. I'll never forget when he learned that his soccer injury left him without the ability to have children."

"That had to have been so terrible for him."

Guido nodded. "When you met him on the yacht

and danced with him, I thought he was the luckiest man alive to meet you after what he'd been through. I also believed he deserved to find an amazing woman like you. But deep inside me I wanted you for myself and was appalled at my feelings of jealousy."

"Oh, Guido—"

"*Oh, Guido* is right! You have to understand that I was at a vulnerable point in my life because I'd decided to buy the soccer team and leave the company for a while. Nothing was a sure thing and I risked alienating my father in a way that might ruin our relationship for good. You talk about floundering while you were at Rini and Alessandra's wedding— so was I."

Before anything more could be said, the Fasten Seat Belt light went on.

"Come on. Let's get back to our seats. We'll resume this talk later."

Dea had wanted secrets from him and she finally had the truth. Now that she knew about his girlfriend from the past and her rejection of him to chase after another celebrity, she understood the war going on inside him where his father was concerned.

When they touched down and got off the plane, he led her to the waiting helicopter and helped her on board. "I promise our flight won't last longer than ten minutes."

Once they were in the air, he used the mic to talk to her. "We're headed for Ischia Island. Have you been there?"

She shook her head. "In my teens Papà drove us past it and the other islands off Naples in the old cruiser, but we never went ashore."

"Then you're in for a treat. We'll be putting down near Serrara Fontana in the mountainous southwest part."

"Does this island have special significance for you?"

"I'll explain in a few minutes," was all he would tell her.

The pilot made a beeline for the highest summit on the island and descended toward an isolated piece of property partially hidden by the vegetation. Soon a helipad appeared and they made a gentle landing.

Guido thanked the pilot before helping Dea to climb out. He grasped her hand and walked her along a path through the grove of chestnut trees. The sound of the rotors grew faint. As they came out the other side to a terraced garden of palms and flowers, he heard Dea's soft gasp.

Her eyes had taken in the two-story pastel-pink villa above the garden with its pool. The ornamental parapets of the balconies overflowed with bougain-villea and hibiscus. "This all looks like something out of a dream." The marvel in her voice told him everything he wanted to know.

He threaded his fingers through hers. "It wasn't like this when I first saw the place sixteen years ago with Rini. We were through diving for the day and decided to explore on rental bikes. After we swam in one of the many hot springs throughout the island, we arrived up here at the top. That's when I saw this wreck of what was clearly once a magnificent villa overlooking the sea, closed up and isolated. Its beauty haunted me."

"You were young to be so affected."

"I agree. Living in Naples all my life, I'd been surrounded by beauty and had traveled to many exotic places in the world. But this spot had such a strong pull on me, I eventually made inquiries of the locals."

"What did they tell you?"

"The original owners had lost their money and were forced to sell. The second owner bought it as an investment but only visited it a few times. Little by little the place fell into more disrepair, and a small portion part of the villa suffered fire damage."

She shook her head, causing her fabulous hair to float around her shoulders. "That's so sad."

He took a deep breath. "Over the years I flew here often. The worse it looked, the more I wanted it. The day it went up for sale again, I bought it and the first thing I did was clear a space for a helipad. Once that was done, I spent all my weekends here restoring the garden and making renovations. To get out of the Naples office and come here to work in the soil was therapeutic for me."

"You did all this by yourself?" She sounded incredulous.

"Most of it, though I did hire locals from time to time."

"When was that?"

"I took possession three years ago."

Her eyes were smiling. "So you could transform it."

"That's one way of putting it."

"Just as you decided to turn a grade-B soccer team into a national champion. I see a pattern here."

He chuckled and drew her into his arms. "But I don't know the outcome of either transformation yet."

"Why not?"

"For the obvious reason that our last three games of the season haven't been played yet. As for the other..." Her mouth was a temptation he couldn't resist. After kissing her long and hard, Guido put his arm around her shoulders and walked her up to the villa. "See for yourself."

He unlocked the main door and drew her inside the large foyer with a curving staircase rising to the next floor and rooms extending on both sides.

Dea walked around the interior, which was devoid of anything but the prepared drywall. She turned to him. "From the outside of the villa, you would never guess this is all unfinished."

He nodded. "It's ready for the right person to take over and create an ambiance of beauty from the flooring to the ceiling."

She eyed him for a moment. "Why not yourself?"

"You've seen my apartment, and I've told you about the one in Naples. This is no bachelor pad and needs the eye of someone with exquisite taste."

"Have you found that person?"

Guido moved closer and put his hands on her shoulders. "How would you like the job?"

Maybe it was a trick of light but he thought her face lost a little color. "Please don't joke about something like that."

"I would never joke about anything this personal. The first time I visited your apartment, I saw a reflection of the real you in everything and loved being there."

"Zia Fulvia helped me decorate when I moved in."

He tightened his fingers around her upper arms and shook her gently. "Why don't you ever take credit for your own genius? Don't you know how wonderful you are?"

"Guido—" Her cheeks filled with color and she pulled away from him.

"It's true. When you were telling me about the opera and how vital the costumes and settings were to making it come alive, I felt *you* come alive. That's the moment I knew I wanted you to see this villa and tell me what needs to be done. I'm sick of apartments and plan to live here for the rest of my life."

"You don't require anyone's help. You've created a masterpiece outside."

"I'm glad you think so, but the real task still awaits me. Come on. After you see the whole house, we'll drive down to the village for lunch and you can tell me what you think."

Not giving her a chance to argue, he grasped her hand and led her up the stairs to see the four bedrooms and bathrooms. The superb view of the Tyrrhenian Sea from the master suite held her gaze for a long time.

A tour of the downstairs included a library and a separate den off the living room. The large kitchen and dining room on the other side of the house produced more cries of delight. He could hear her mind working and knew her imagination had taken over.

A detached garage in the same Mediterranean style with a tiled roof stood behind the villa. Along with the gardening equipment, Guido kept a truck and his Alfa Romeo Spider convertible locked up there. He helped her get in his vintage sports car and they took off down the winding road. The smell of roses and jasmine hung heavy in the air. The woman seated next to him had no clue what she meant to him. Not yet...

I'm sick of apartments and plan to live here for the rest of my life. This is no bachelor pad and needs the eye of someone with exquisite taste. How would you like the job?

"We're coming into Sant'Angelo, an old fishing village." Guido's deep male voice curled through Dea's insides. "My sailboat is moored there in the harbor. One day I'll take you out and we'll sail around the island."

"Which one is it?"

"The white and blue one, which isn't much help, since so many boats are the same."

She laughed. "This little town is a panoply of white, blue and ochre houses all pressed together in a symphony of color. I've lived by the water all my life, but our family's island has no color, just a dark stone castle."

He threw her a glance. "The severity has a beauty all its own."

"I agree, but this paradise dazzles the eye. The impossible yellows and pinks of the flowers make me think you live in heaven."

"Today I'm there."

She felt the same way as he slowed down and parked the car in a tiny space only someone as daring as Guido would have tried to navigate. He levered himself from the driver's side and came around to open her door. "In a few minutes you're going to taste pasta *arrabbiata* with a spicy kick that is out of this world. Emanuela's is right here on the beach."

For a little while Dea let go of her fear that he couldn't trust her feelings for him and inhaled the experience of being with Guido like this, a man whose background she was only beginning to understand, a man she already loved with all her heart and soul.

The food and wine turned out to be divine. Throughout their meal, his dark blue eyes wandered over her, causing every nerve in her body to throb with desire.

Following a tasty treat of raspberry gelato, they walked back to the car and took a drive around the island on the main road.

Traveling to the quaint, picturesque villages filled her with delight. He was better than any tour director or history teacher. He talked about the local legend of

the giant living in the volcanic rock and the tufa lime-
stone deposits built up around the fumaroles and spas.

Dea learned the island was shaped like a trapezoid
and housed sixty-two thousand people. The larger
towns sold everything imaginable. In Casamicciola
she bought some small ceramic tiles of Ischia for her
mother and sister. It was after five when Guido drove
through the hamlet of Ciglio, close to the villa. They
bought sausage rolls in puff pastry and fruit tarts to
take with them.

After arriving back at the villa, Guido parked the
car in the garage. Then he led her to a wrought iron
bench by the pool, where they ate their picnic. The
helicopter would be coming shortly, but Dea didn't
want to think about that yet.

"Do you know one of the meanings of *alfresco*?"
His eyes gleamed with mischief.

"Besides eating outside?" She smiled. "This garden is no prison. You know very well you've created
a work of art out here."

"Then will you do me a favor and think about my
proposition? While you're getting the costumes ready
for *Don Giovanni*, will you picture the villa in your
mind and tell me what kind of floors you envision
here? A color scheme? Would you work up a rough
draft that will point me in the right direction?"

She swallowed the rest of her pastry. *Stick to him
like glue*, Alessandra had advised her. She had to
prove to him how important he was to her.

"I'm flattered that you want my opinion. Let me
think about it and I'll get back to you."

A look of relief crossed over his striking features. "That's all I ask. I'd like to fly you here again next Friday night after work if you don't have other plans. We can stay over in Ciglio, then spend Saturday here. I'll have to get back to Rome Saturday night because the team is flying to Siena first thing Sunday morning."

"I'll try to get off on the dot of five. Maybe I can drive to the airport from work and meet you at the plane to save time. As it is, we won't get here until nightfall."

They both heard the helicopter coming. Her disappointment that they had to leave this paradise was killing her.

"I'll be counting the hours until we can be here together again, Dea." He cupped her face with both hands and kissed her mouth. "Umm. I can still taste the cherries on your lips."

He kissed her thoroughly before they walked through the trees to board the helicopter. As it rose in the air, she felt like her heart had been wrenched from her body. The villa got smaller until she could see the island where she'd known such great happiness. Dea couldn't bear to go back to her apartment. But she needed to get hold of herself so he wouldn't know how much this day had meant to her.

On the flight back to Rome, she told him one of her ideas for decorating the villa while they were seated in the club compartment of the plane. "When we were in Casamicciola, we passed a store with the most wonderful ceramic floor tiles in various shades from white to cream."

"You noticed all that?"

"Well, you *did* ask me to think about it. I couldn't help but see your main floor and walls as an extension of the outdoors where light sweeps through the interior, even up the staircase.

"One of the bedroom floors upstairs could contain a soft pink pigment to reflect the exterior of the villa. Maybe another bedroom could be done in a subtle gray-blue. Your kitchen would be gorgeous with hints of a lemon motif in the wall tiles to reflect the astounding yellow of the flowers on the island."

His brows lifted. "Wall tiles… You've already envisioned that in your mind?"

She smiled. "You'd be surprised what's going on in there." Dea had already designed a nursery for his children. Her thoughts wouldn't stop. "It's your fault, you know."

A low laugh came out of him. He sounded happy, in fact happier than she'd ever known him to be. This blissful state continued until they landed in Rome and he drove them to her apartment.

"Just pull up in front and let me out. I know you have a game tomorrow and I don't want to keep you."

"You're sure?"

That one question threw her for a loop. Dea had thought he would insist on seeing her inside so he could kiss her senseless. He'd spoiled her today. Now she was a mess, wanting so much more. *You're being selfish again.* He had a huge day ahead of him.

"Good luck tomorrow, Guido." She undid her seat belt to kiss his cheek before getting out of the car with her small souvenirs.

"I'll call you tomorrow night if it isn't too late."

"Don't worry about that." Dea shut the door and hurried inside the building to her apartment. He hadn't asked her if she wanted to attend the soccer match. What did that mean?

Once she'd showered and climbed into bed, she lay there wide-awake reliving her incredible day. Was it another test to see if she cared about him enough to show up uninvited? Should she do the unexpected, as Alessandra had suggested?

Dea wrestled with that question for a long time. Finally she concluded that since he'd asked her advice on how to decorate the villa, she'd take her chances and go to the match. She had to see him again or she wouldn't be able to make it to Monday when she had to go to work.

Guido, Guido. I love you so much I'm in pain.

CHAPTER SEVEN

GUIDO AND SERGIO sat in his private suite next to the press box to watch the game. Maybe thirty minutes had gone by when he heard his phone ring. When he saw the caller ID, he picked up.

"What's going on, Mario?"

"This is important. Someone has asked to be let into your suite, but it has to be all right with you."

He could only think of one person he wanted with him today, but that was a dream that wouldn't happen. "If you're referring to Rinieri Montanari or his wife, Alessandra, you know they always have an automatic entrée."

"I'm talking about the gorgeous supermodel who was here last week with friends."

"You're serious—"

"*Sì*. I swear she's here at the ticket booth."

Guido's breath caught in his throat. He hadn't expected her to show up today.

Last night he'd been tempted to ask her to come to the game and spend the rest of the night with him, but he'd held back, waiting for her to suggest it. When she didn't, he'd suffered disappointment.

As he and Sergio had discussed many times, few women—barring those who played the game or had a family member on the team—could get into soccer in a big way. But Dea had been supportive from day one. Maybe she was different.

"Boss? Shall I bring her up?"

"Please," he said when he could find his voice.

Sergio stared at him after he clicked off. "What's wrong? Is Dante's leg still bothering him?"

He hoped not. "We're about to have an unexpected visitor."

"I thought you said your father would never come to the stadium to watch a game."

"You've got the wrong gender."

"Your mother?"

"Wrong again." He got to his feet.

"Ah… Then it must be your secret woman."

Sergio never let up. Guido moved to the door and opened it to watch for her. In a moment he saw her walking in the corridor alongside Mario.

The dark blue short-sleeved dress with small red poppies Dea was wearing hugged her figure, then flared from the waist to the knee. With every step, the material danced around her beautiful legs, imitating the flounce of her hair, which she wore down, the way he liked it. Talk about his heart failing him!

"Dea—"

Her searching gaze fused with his. "I hope it's all

right." The slight tremor in her voice betrayed her fear that she wasn't welcome. If she only knew...

"You've had an open invitation since we met." Nodding his thanks to Mario, he put his arm around her shoulders and drew her inside the suite. Sergio slipped out of the room and closed the door so they could be alone.

He slid his hands into her hair. "You're the most beautiful sight this man has ever seen." With uncontrolled hunger he lowered his mouth to hers and began to devour her. Over the announcer's voice and the roar of the crowd, he heard her little moans of pleasure as their bodies merged and they drank deeply.

When she swayed in his arms, he half carried her over to the couch, where they could give in to their frenzied needs. She smelled heavenly. One kiss grew into another until she became his entire world. He'd never known a feeling like this and lost track of time and place.

"Do you know what you do to me?" he whispered against her lips with feverish intensity.

"I came for the same reason."

Her admission pulled him all the way under. Once in a while the roar of the crowd filled the room, but that didn't stop him from twining his legs with hers. He desired a closeness they couldn't achieve as long as their clothes separated them.

"I want you, *bellissima*. I want you all night long. Do you understand what I'm saying?"

Before he heard her answer, the noise from the crowd became earsplitting. Within a minute someone unlocked the door and burst in. "Boss? I've been trying to reach you. Though we won the game, Dante's leg may be broken. You're needed in the locker room. *Viene subito!*"

Dante… The game was over… For the last hour he'd been so caught up with Dea he hadn't noticed the passing of time.

After being jerked back from rapture he hadn't thought possible, his brain was slow to digest what Sergio had just told him.

Dea had more presence of mind. She eased herself out of his arms and got to her feet before he did. He stood there for a minute, raking one hand through his ruffled hair. "What happened?"

"He fell hard on his sore leg after getting kicked."

Dea put a comforting hand on his arm. "Go to him, Guido. If you can, come to my apartment later. If not, call me." In the next breath, she ran out the door before he could detain her.

Much as he wanted to go after her, he knew his duty was to Dante. Dea hadn't wanted to leave him; otherwise she wouldn't have told him to come to her place later. Loving her for her consideration, he started down the hall. By now the team doctor would have looked their star player over.

It wasn't until he was on his way into the locker room and saw Dante's family that he realized those hours with Dea had swept him away to a different world where nothing else had mattered. Not even his team. After she'd arrived, he hadn't watched a second of the game. Worse, he hadn't known of their victory until Sergio barged in.

It would all have been taped for Guido, but the news was bittersweet. Only two more matches before the end of the season. They'd have to play them without their star, Dante. For Sergio this had to be déjà vu. Ten years ago he'd suffered an injury that had knocked him out of competition for good. Guido had to pray Dante would heal well enough to play again.

This was the downside of being a team owner. His job was to encourage the rest of the team to carry on to a national victory. Realizing what he had to do tonight, he knew he wouldn't be able to get over to Dea's until long after she went to bed.

After he watched the ambulance take Dante to the hospital, he congratulated the team and had a short pep talk with them. Once the guys left, he phoned Dea. She answered on the second ring.

"Guido. How is Dante?"

"He's gone to the hospital. I'll know more by tomorrow morning."

"You sound exhausted. Don't come over tonight. It's late. Go home to bed and if you can, concentrate on your latest win. You're almost there."

"I don't know. Without Dante, our strength has been reduced."

"I don't think that's true. You have other players who will step up. One of them will realize this is their opportunity to become a new star for the team. Sometimes wonderful things come out of tragedy."

If she was speaking from experience, then she'd

learned a great deal about life. Her fighting spirit was exactly what he needed right now. "Thank you for those words. They mean more than you could know."

"I'm happy you said that. Here I was afraid that my arrival during the game prevented you from watching the rest of it and you resented me."

He let out an exasperated sigh. "What I resented was having to let you go at all. May I have a rain check for tomorrow evening? I'll bring takeout to your apartment after work and we'll watch the game we missed. How does that sound?"

"I'd love it, but tomorrow evening my aunt will be in Rome and we're going out to dinner with Juliana." He had to swallow the bad news that they wouldn't be able to see each other as soon as he'd wanted. "Maybe the next night? I'll show you some of my ideas for your villa. They bombarded me all night long. Where do you keep all your trophies?"

Her mind leaped around and fascinated him so much that laughter escaped his lips despite his disappointment. "My parents' villa."

"How many do you have?"

Guido shook his head. "I don't know."

"Enough to fill a room?"

"Why?"

"You know that little nook off the den? It would be a great place to keep them. Kind of like your own museum. I can see a wallpaper motif of a real lion head with the words *Cuor di Leone* above it. On one side could be family pictures of your parents. On the

other, pictures of you at different ages to immortal-
ize the Rossano name.

"I can hear what you're thinking," she added, "so
here's the plan. You could have double doors hung
that locked and couldn't be opened unless you used
a remote. I know how modest you are, so if you don't
want anyone else to see it, then there's no problem."

He was so touched by her words he had trouble
finding the right response. "I can see you think big-
ger than life."

"It comes from living in a castle with the enormous
painting of Queen Joanna dominating the foyer. We
Caracciolos can't think any other way."

His throat had swelled with emotion. "I'll call you
Tuesday and we'll make plans. Miss me, Dea." He
hung up and headed to his car. The next time he was
with her, he was going to have the most important
discussion of his life with her.

Miss me, Dea.

She'd heard the huskiness in his tone. Didn't he
know she wouldn't be able to breathe until they were
together again?

Luckily Dea was kept so busy at work the time
flew until she went out for an enjoyable dinner with
her aunt and Juliana Monday evening. During the
meal her mentor praised Dea's work. She also announced that they'd be working at the opera house
for the next three evenings while rehearsals for *Don
Giovanni* were going on. The opera would open the
following week.

Exciting as that prospect would be in the professional sense, it meant Dea wouldn't be able to see Guido until Friday. When his phone call came Tuesday afternoon, she had to tell him news that was hard on her too. "But I promise that nothing will keep me from meeting you at the airport on Friday at four thirty."

A full half minute of silence met her ears before he said, "I don't know if I can last that long."

"I feel the same way," she admitted, but something else was bothering him, evidenced by some nuance in his voice. "How's Dante?"

"He's out for the season."

"I'm so sorry."

"He received flowers at the hospital, among them some roses with a card that was signed by Dea Loti and said, 'A fan who is wishing you back to health as soon as possible.' Do you have any idea how honored he felt?"

"Good. He got them!"

"All the guys have come in and out of his room and read your card. Now his celebrity status has shot through the roof. Sergio and Mario are green with envy."

"Guido…those flowers were meant to cheer you up too."

"You succeeded. How am I supposed to wait until Friday?"

"The same way I am. Work, work, work."

"There's steel beneath all that beauty."

"And a warrior lives inside you! Your team is

going to be superb at their next match, all because of their legendary owner."

"The things you say," he whispered. "If you were with me right now…"

"We'll be together on Friday. I'm staying positive for you. *A presto*, Guido." She hung up before blurting that she loved him, but that day was coming soon.

At four fifteen on Friday, Dea arrived at the airport by taxi, so eager to see Guido her cheeks were flushed and she thought she might be running a temperature. She hurried out on the tarmac to the section for the private planes. In the distance she saw the Scatto Roma jet. The door was open and the staircase had been placed against it.

He was here! She ran all the way with her overnight bag and raced up the steps straight into his arms. Guido put her bag down and buried his face in her hair. "I saw you coming. Thank heaven you're early. I couldn't have stood to wait another minute."

"Neither could I!" She pressed her mouth to his, kissing him so hungrily she almost knocked him over like she had playing soccer with him. Dea was no longer the same person. This man Guido—the love of her life—was eating her alive while he carried her all the way to his bedroom. For the next while she lost cognizance of her world. Overwhelmed with the pleasure he gave her, she hardly realized a voice had sounded over the plane's PA system.

"Signor Rossano? Do you wish to take off now?"

On a groan, Guido lifted his head and pulled out his phone. "We're ready."

"Bene."

His blue eyes were glazed with desire as he looked down at her. "We have to go to the club compartment."

"You shouldn't have brought me back here."

"I couldn't do anything else." He snatched another kiss from her lips and helped her to stand. Her hair was a complete mess and her lipstick had long since disappeared. She felt herself wobble on the way to the front of the jet, where they strapped themselves in their seats.

His eyes never left hers as the plane taxied out to the runway. Soon the engines screamed and they lifted off into the early evening sun. Once they'd achieved cruising speed, the steward brought them dinner.

"To shorten the time we're in the air, we're flying directly to Ischia and will drive a rental car to our hotel in Ciglio. How does that sound?"

She finished munching on some bruschetta. "I think you already know."

"Tell me how things are going at the opera."

"It's a whole other world. You can't imagine how exciting it is to see the singers get dressed in their costumes. All our hard work is on display, but I have to tell you one funny thing. Gina wasn't given the right dimensions for Leporello's jacket. When he tried it on, his considerable belly prevented it from closing. Gina and I tried not to explode from laughter."

Guido flashed her a broad smile.

"Juliana saved the day by finding a red scarf that she wrapped around him so the front edges would lie flat. When he reached for notes, we were all afraid the scarf would burst, but it didn't. Her ability to innovate at the last second makes her the queen of costume designers."

"I'm looking forward to seeing the opera performed."

"Me too. It starts next week."

"You'll have to show me the costumes you designed."

"I only helped."

"Now who's being modest?"

She finished her coffee. "Do you think your team is ready for the game in Siena?"

His brows furrowed. "They're going to have to be, but Drago can only do so much."

"One of the other players will step up. Have no fear."

"You really believe that, don't you?"

Heavens—in chinos and a sport shirt, the man was so incredibly attractive with that dark blond hair that she couldn't help staring. "Yes. They want you to be proud of them. You're their hero."

He made a protesting sound. "You don't know that."

"Oh, yes, I do. I'll never forget the look of worship in Aldo's eyes when he met you in person. Your team's feelings for you have to be a hundred times stronger."

"Did I ever tell you how good you are for me?"

"I don't know how you can say that when I caused you to miss watching an hour of the game last Sunday evening."

"There's a lot more I want to say on that subject, but I'll wait until we're completely alone."

How wonderful that sounded. A minute later the steward removed their trays and told them they'd be landing soon. Dea sat back, aching to get Guido all to herself. Within three minutes the Fasten Seat Belt sign flicked on and they began their descent. In the dying rays of the sun, Ischia rose up to greet them.

A rental car was waiting on the tarmac. Guido loaded them inside and drove them out to the main road. Guido pampered her to the point she felt sorry for every woman who would never know what it was like to be with a fabulous man like him.

It soon became clear that the island was overrun with tourists. She wished they didn't have to stay at a crowded hotel tonight, no matter how charming it might be. "We should have brought sleeping bags we could put down at the villa."

"On those hard subfloors? Not exactly my idea of comfort, but I'm living for the day when it's ready for occupation."

Dea eyed him covertly. "There's still your sailboat. We could pick up some goodies in the village and sleep on board."

She heard a harsh intake of breath. "You must have been reading my mind. I wanted to take you there in the first place, but it's intimate. Contrary to what you've probably heard about me, I'm not the kind of man who sleeps with every woman I fancy. I would never treat you that way."

"You thought I'd feel more comfortable staying at a hotel with adjoining rooms?"

"I'm trying hard to be a gentleman with you."

"Please try harder not to be."

His deep unexpected laughter filled the car's interior. "There's no other woman in the world like you, Dea. How did I get so lucky?"

"I've been saying that to myself about you ever since our own little soccer game." She ached with love for him. "I'm afraid I'm not known for my subtlety. To be honest, I've never been to bed with a man."

"That's what I thought."

"Does it show so much? Is that why you haven't tried to take advantage of me?"

"A woman who knows her value is more desirable than you can imagine."

"Well, I hate to ruin that image you have of me because it's all I can think about when I'm with you."

"Now she tells me."

His teasing was driving her crazy. "Surely at this point you must realize that if I thought you were a true playboy out to use me, we would never have made it this far."

"I think that's a compliment of sorts. But in case you've got the entirely wrong opinion about me, I'll be honest too. Over the years I've had a few very short-term intimate relationships with women. None since my birthday last year, however."

The birthday on the yacht... "That night changed history for both of us, Guido."

"You're right. That was the night my world underwent an upheaval from which I've never recovered and don't want to." He reached over and put a hand on her thigh. Through the fabric of her cotton pants, she felt his touch electrify her body. "If you really want to spend the night on the boat, there's nothing I want more. We'll head straight to Sant'Angelo now."

"I'd love it," she answered in a trembling voice. "But if you've already made reservations, I—"

"Don't worry about it. I'll cancel them now."

To her delight he pulled out his cell phone and made the call, ensuring a perfect night. All week she'd imagined them alone and away from other people with no pressure. It looked like she was going to get her heart's desire, and she preened like Alfredo when he found a spot in the sun.

Within an hour they'd picked up food and had walked over to the pier. They planned to go sailing in the morning. Dea had brought her bikini in case they decided to swim and sunbathe. But they would stay right here for tonight.

Guido led her to his one-man sailboat moored in its own slip. When she saw the name of it painted on the side, she let out a cry and stared at him. "The *Bona Dea*?"

He nodded. "The *Good Goddess*."

Her eyes rounded. "How long have you owned this boat?"

"I bought it off a fisherman two years ago. He'd

owned it for fifteen years and had named it for the ancient Roman goddess of fertility, *your* namesake, as it turns out."

"I don't believe it!"

"Truth is stranger than fiction. I was in love with your name long before we met. It just took meeting you in the flesh to complete my entrancement."

CHAPTER EIGHT

DEA BLUSHED AND climbed on board. It was no surprise to Guido she knew her way around a boat. She'd lived by the water all her life, even if she hadn't learned to water ski until he'd helped her.

Together they went below with their overnight bags and freshened up. She helped him make the bed with clean sheets and a blanket from the cupboard. After pulling out an extra quilt, he took it and the pillows up on deck so they could be comfortable.

"Come here." He propped himself against them and drew her down so she lay against him on the padded side of the boat. It rocked gently in the water. Once he'd covered them with the quilt, they enjoyed some of the nuts and chocolate they'd bought.

The lights of the village reflected in her eyes. "It's like looking at wonderland, Guido."

He kissed her temple. "You like this place?"

Dea nestled closer. "What a question."

"I've spent many nights right here on the water."

"I can see why."

"Can you imagine yourself living here?"

"That's not a trick question. Or is it?" She lifted her head to look at him. Her glossy hair drifted across his cheek. "What are you saying?"

He kissed every part of her face. "Do I really have to answer that?"

"Guido—" By now she was sitting up. Her body had gone taut with emotion. "Please don't tease me. Not about this. I couldn't take it."

His expression grew serious. "I'm in love with you, Dea. So in love that I never want to be apart from you."

"You are?" she asked in a shaky voice. Tears glistened in her eyes.

"Do you really need convincing, my love? I want to marry you right away and spend the rest of my life on this island with you. I want so many things. I'm bursting with the need to tell you. Forgive me if I'm moving too fast, but I can't help it. I've loved you for too long believing there was no hope."

She put her hands on his shoulders. "I've been waiting, dying for you to tell me. I was afraid I might never hear the words. I'm madly in love with you, Guido."

"I thought maybe I had a chance with you when I saw a poster of me in your bedroom at the apartment."

"You *saw* it?"

He nodded. "I knew you'd bought two posters. The evidence gave me hope, something I badly needed."

"Oh, darling. After our day on the water with Alessandra and Rini, I knew I was truly falling in love for the first time in my life."

"It happened to me when you tackled me."

"But *I* didn't know that! You left the castle that morning before I could say a final goodbye to you."

"You know why. I knew it was too soon to ask for all your passion."

"And all my truth," she reminded him. "You think I didn't want the same thing?" Dea gave him another fervent kiss and shook him gently. "When I discovered you'd already gone that Sunday morning, I felt such pain go through me that I knew you'd taken my heart with you. What if I never saw you again? I was terrified until you called me to go to lunch."

"*Adorata*, I've lived in terror since that night on the yacht. If I couldn't have you, I didn't want another woman. For a while I was out of my mind fearing I would never be able to have my heart's desire."

She kissed him hard. "No more talk about the past. I want to be your wife, Guido. I've already designed our whole villa, complete with the most adorable nursery you ever saw in your life. We're going to have children to keep both sets of grandparents busy. Is this your official proposal?"

The lovelight in her eyes blinded him. "It's official, *bellissima*." He reached in his pocket and put a diamond solitaire on her ring finger.

"It fits perfectly!" She squealed. "Oh, Guido—you've had this all along?" She hugged him around the neck with the same strength she'd shown playing soccer. "It's gorgeous! *You're* gorgeous!"

"So are you. I love you." He covered her mouth with his own, hardly able to believe that she was going to be his wife after he'd lived through so much agony. Later, when he let her up for breath, she said, "Let's go below so I can show you how much you mean to me."

"Dea, before we both lose complete control, we need to talk about our future." He grasped her hands and kissed the palms. "You've made me the happiest man alive. To know I'm going to be your husband is such a privilege. I want to do everything right."

"What do you mean?"

"Just that I want our wedding night to be the first time we make love. After what you've told me, it's my way of honoring you."

"But—"

"No buts." He pressed another kiss to her lips. "I want to be worthy of you."

"Guido, of course you're worthy! We *love* each other. I don't understand."

"I need you to love me always and be proud of me. Especially of what I'll be doing in the future."

Her brows knit together. "I *am* proud of you and whatever you do. You have to know that!"

"You say that now, and I love you for being so supportive of me. But the owner of a soccer team isn't a befitting profession for the husband of Count Caracciolo's princess daughter."

"What?"

"You know it isn't! Hear me out, *squisita*. I couldn't sleep thinking about you last night. I couldn't wait for us to be together so I could ask you to marry me. The fact that you've said yes changes everything."

"In what way?"

"I'm no prospect at the moment. Certainly no father's idea of the right kind of son-in-law. My father never liked it that I fell in love with soccer."

"But that doesn't mean he doesn't love you with all his heart and support whatever decision you make. Where is all this insecurity coming from? Are you afraid I'll leave you if you stick with soccer? I can see that I'm right."

He shook his head. "Whatever the reason, this comes from wanting to take care of you the best way I can and be an example to the children we'll have. So I've decided to sell the team at the end of the season whether we're victorious or not. It's only two weeks away. Sergio and Mario have always been interested in buying me out if I chose not to go on."

"You don't mean it! You love the soccer world!"

"Not the way I love you and the children I want to have with you. Tomorrow I'll inform my father and grandfather that I'm coming back to work for the company. They'll be ecstatic."

"I'm sure they will, but it's you I'm worried about. You left the company last year because you felt stifled and needed to do something of your very own. We've already talked about this. I thought we were going sailing tomorrow and talking more about plans for the villa. I was thinking we could put in an herb garden at the side of the house."

"I love all your ideas, Dea, and want to do everything with you. But this is too important to put off.

If you don't mind, I want us to go back to Rome in the morning."

"Stop, Guido. Can't you hear what you're saying? You haven't worked for the company in almost a year. How can you be sure it's what you want to do?"

"I'm very sure now that I know I'm going to have a loving wife to take care of for the rest of our lives. Nothing's more important to me than you."

"Being CEO won't give you the freedom you've had as a soccer-team owner. Think about the way you felt when you decided to leave the company and do something that made you feel alive."

He crushed her to him. "I didn't have you in my life then. I want our lives to have stability."

"But you have that being the owner of Scatto Roma."

"It's not the same thing. Trust me."

"If your team wins the national championship, you might feel very differently about things then. Give it a little more time, darling. How can you think about all this when you're flying to Siena Sunday morning to play an important match?"

"I'll be able to fit everything in." He pulled her down next to him again. "After we get back to Rome, I'll fly to Naples. My father will be so elated he'll plan to call a meeting of the board and things will be put into motion to make me CEO. I want all that in play before we tell either of our parents that we're getting married."

She lay against him, much quieter than before. "Then I'd better not wear this engagement ring around anyone yet."

He kissed her neck. "It'll be our secret for two more weeks, then we can shout it to the world. For now I'll know you have it and that you've promised to be my wife."

"Tell me what it is you'll do as CEO."

"Find new markets for new ships. The business is constantly evolving."

"How do you go about doing that?"

"Right now I'd rather talk about you and your work. When do you graduate?"

"In June. My internship with Juliana will be over."

"Do you think she'll let you go on working with her?"

"I wouldn't dream of asking her. I need to prove myself and will have to apply elsewhere. It may take time to find a company that will hire me. One day I hope to build a reputation for myself."

"You don't have to wait to do that. I'll set you up in your own business and opera companies will flock to you."

"That's very generous of you, darling, but this I have to do myself. Gina is in the same boat. We're both watching out for each other. While I wait for a bite, I'll be helping you work on the villa."

"Before that we'll be planning our wedding. I already know where you want to be married."

"Since you're an only child, maybe your parents would love to see you married in Naples at your church."

"You're going to be the bride, Dea. It'll be your day and your choice."

"You mean that?"

He drew her closer. "How can you even ask me that question?"

"Then I think it would be lovely to let them give you the wedding of their dreams. They don't have a daughter. My parents have twin girls and they've already had the joy of helping Alessandra plan her wedding."

"It was magnificent," he murmured. "The Archbishop of Taranto even officiated."

"You've told me of your mother's sorrow and your father's pain because he knew she'd wanted more children. When you tell him his plan worked to find you a wife, I have a feeling your parents will get a new lease on life and plan something magnificent too."

Guido looked into her eyes. "You don't have a selfish bone in your delectable body. More than ever I know I don't deserve you, but I'm going to try from here on out to be all the things you want me to be. *Ti amo*, Dea. *Ti amo*."

With Guido's declaration of love, he'd sent Dea the message she'd been waiting for all her life, and eventually she fell asleep. But in the middle of the night she awakened disoriented. It took her a minute to realize she was on the sailboat with him.

Careful not to disturb this man she loved to distraction, she eased out of his arms and got to her feet. The moonlight picked out his striking features and caught the facets of her diamond. Tonight he'd asked her to marry him. On her finger was the proof, yet during her sleep something had bothered her so badly she'd come wide-awake.

She needed another talk with her sister, but that couldn't happen until they flew back to Rome. The night was cool so she went downstairs and slept under the blanket until she heard Guido call to her.

"I'm right here, darling!" She slid off the bed and started up the stairs. They met halfway and Guido swept her in his arms. His kiss was to die for.

"Where did you go?" He sounded alarmed.

Dea rubbed his hard jaw. "Umm. You have a beard."

"Don't change the subject."

"I guess I'm so excited at the thought of marrying you I woke up during the night. You were sleeping peacefully. I didn't want to disturb you, so I came down here and went back to sleep."

"When I couldn't find you, I—"

She hushed the rest of his sentence with her mouth. "It's going to be fun getting to know all the fascinating little things about each other."

He cupped her face. "Except when you scare the daylights out of me."

"What did you think happened?" Dea wanted to understand him.

Guido held her close. "You don't want to know. I feared someone might have come by and tried to drag you off."

"Oh, darling, I'm so sorry."

"No. *I* am for not insisting we go downstairs last night, where we could be totally private and I could better protect you. If you'll gather your things, we'll get going. We can shower on the plane and have breakfast."

She smiled. "Don't shave. I like your five o'clock shadow."

His eyes darkened with emotion. "I don't know if I can wait to marry you."

"You're going to be exciting to live with. Already I know you're an impatient man. It will be a challenge to keep up with you. Come on. Let's get going. I can tell you're hungry. I think there are a few more nuts left on deck to tide you over."

She gave him a kiss on the cheek, then hurried back down to the bathroom to gather her things and straighten the blanket on the bed. Guido brought the quilt and pillows downstairs and put them in the cupboard.

"Pretty soon we'll be getting a lot of use out of that," he said, glancing at the bed.

Her heart raced. "Don't make promises you can't keep." On that bold note she dashed out of the room and up the stairs with her overnight case. His deep laughter preceded him on deck.

Before they got in the rental car, she took off her ring and slipped it in her purse. It wouldn't do if the steward or the pilot saw her wearing it. Secrets always had a way of getting out. Word would somehow get back to Guido's family.

On the way to the airport she brushed her hair and put on lipstick. Guido watched her out of the corner of his eye. "You're going to be my wife, but I still can't believe I'm marrying my fantasy."

"I love you so much. It seems too wonderful to be true."

His hands tightened on the steering wheel. "I'd like to take you to Naples with me. I hope you understand why I need to go alone first."

"I do."

"I probably won't get back to Rome until midnight and then I'll have to be up at dawn."

"Guido? How would you feel if I flew to Siena to watch the game with you?"

"Much as I'd love it, when we're the visiting team I can't see to your needs or make you comfortable."

She could tell what he was trying to do. He had no idea how much this was hurting her. To her grief, there was no dissuading him from his plans. "Then I'll watch it on TV."

"As soon as it's over, I'll phone you and we'll make plans to spend Monday night together."

Once they boarded the plane and were in the air, Guido disappeared long enough to shower and change so he'd be able to fly directly to Naples from the airport in Rome. Dea decided to wait until she got home to her apartment to shower and wash her hair.

The steward served them a delicious breakfast. Guido asked her to show him some of her drawings for the villa. She got them out of her case and they pored over everything. He had his own ideas, of course, but loved most everything she'd suggested except for the *Cuor di Leone* motif.

"That's too over the top, *bellissima*." He squeezed her hand across the table. "Have I hurt your feelings?"

"Yes, but I'll find a way to live with it. In fact I'll put that poster of you on the door of our new walk-in closet, where I can indulge my fantasy about you."

Too soon the seat belt light flashed. They were getting ready to land. This would be their first separation as an engaged couple, but she could tell Guido's mind was in a dozen different places. He was a man on a mission. The wrong one, as far as she was concerned.

When they'd taxied to a stop, Guido walked her out of the plane and down the steps to a waiting limo he'd arranged for her. He helped her in the back with her case and told the driver where to take her.

"The next time we're together, we'll plan our wedding. One more game a week from Sunday, and then we'll tell our families. *Miss me*." He planted a fierce kiss on her mouth before shutting the door.

That was the second time he'd said that to her. Did he honestly think she wouldn't? Didn't he know yet what he meant to her?

She gave him a little wave. The limo drove away before he could see moisture bathing her cheeks. It didn't take long for Dea to get into her apartment. She hoped no one had seen her tear-ravaged face.

The minute she was safely inside, she opened her purse and put the ring in her jewelry case. With that done, she pulled out her phone and flung herself on the bed to call Alessandra.

Please be home. Please answer.

Five rings and her voice mail came on. Of course it

did. On a Saturday she and Rini had to be out somewhere with the baby. Dea asked her to phone her back
when she could without leaving a reason for the call.

This ought to have been the happiest day of her
life, but as it wore on, her pain grew heavier. A trip
to work out in the gym didn't relieve it. All she could
think about was Guido's reason for flying to Naples
today.

She came back to the apartment to shower and
wash her hair. The rest of the day was taken up when
Daphne Butelli, the friend who she'd modeled with,
phoned. Daphne wanted to meet up, so they decided
to see a film and get dinner after. The distraction
didn't help her mental state. She came back to the
apartment still filled with anxiety.

While she was watching the news on TV, her phone
rang. *At last*, she thought when she saw the caller ID.

"Alessandra?"

"Hi, Dea. I'm so sorry not to have gotten back to
you until now. We spent the day with Rini's father
in Naples. It was his birthday. Carlo and his family
came too. As usual we had to take so much stuff for
Brazzo I forgot my phone. Until we got back home
tonight, I didn't realize you'd called me this morning."

"Please don't apologize. Is Rini close by?"

"No. He's in the den taking care of business he
didn't get done today. Are you all right?"

"Yes."

"No, you're not. I can hear it in your voice."

"I'm afraid Rini will walk in on our conversation."

"This is about Guido, right?"

A sad laugh escaped. "Who else?" The tears started again.

"We're safe for a while. Talk to me."

"I'll make this short. In case Rini surprises you, please don't react to what I'm going to tell you and don't tell him anything after you hang up. Make something up. This is for your ears only."

"I promise."

"We spent the night on his sailboat in Ischia. He asked me to marry him and gave me a beautiful diamond ring. But he doesn't want anyone to know we're engaged yet. He plans to sell his soccer team after his last game a week from tomorrow.

"In the meantime, he flew to Naples today to tell his father he's going back to the shipping lines and will accept the position as CEO. When all that is accomplished, then we'll announce our wedding plans."

"What you've just told me has me jumping out of my skin for joy, so why are you so unhappy?"

Dea sank down on the side of the bed. "Because when I see Guido on Monday night, I'm giving back the ring."

A long silence followed. "What am I missing?"

"Guido's afraid I'll leave him."

"I'm not following."

"Maybe this will help." She told her sister about Guido's insecurity where his father was concerned. "He said that the owner of a soccer team isn't a befitting profession for the husband of Count Caracciolo's princess daughter."

"He actually *said* that?"

"Oh, yes."

She heard her sister groan. "I can't believe it."

"Neither can I. Deep in his psyche he thinks he has to work for his father to prove his own worth."

"Oh, Dea, I don't know what to say."

"You're not alone. A year ago he left the shipping business to buy the soccer team. He loves what he does *now*. There's excitement in him. I'm afraid he'll lose all that by giving it up. He's only doing it because of me, Alessandra, and what he thinks his father expects of him. I can't live with him knowing he's giving up what he loves most."

"No. I couldn't, either."

"I'm glad you agree with me." Given the turbulent, painful history between Dea and her sister, only Alessandra could understand her reasoning. "If I return the ring on Monday night, no harm will have been done. No one will ever have to know he proposed and it will all be over before any decisions he's made are final. Then he'll be free to do what he really wants."

"But he wants you."

"He won't want me, not when he knows why I can't keep the ring. And I've made another decision."

"What's that?"

"Tomorrow I'm going to send out résumés over the internet to places needing period costume designers for either the opera or the theater. If it means moving to England or France for a time, I know it will be a good thing. My career is important to me and I'm not going to let this set me back."

"I love you, Dea, and I'm behind you a thousand percent."

"Thank you for listening. I needed to say it out loud." She appreciated her sister not trying to reason with her or talk her out of anything. "I love you too. Take care. Good night."

CHAPTER NINE

I⊤ WAS TEN to twelve Sunday night when Guido arrived back at his apartment. The fabulous game results were in. Team Scatto Roma: 2—Siena: 0

A forward on the opposition side had developed a bad case of stomach flu and couldn't play. Fate was with Guido's team despite Dante's fractured leg. One more win next Sunday and the national championship would be theirs.

Guido quickly phoned Dea. He had so much to tell her, he couldn't wait to hear her voice. But disappointment flooded him when his call went to her voice mail. He'd have to wait until tomorrow to talk to her.

Exhausted from virtually no sleep in the last twenty-four hours, he passed out the minute his head hit the pillow. He woke up at eight and checked his phone. Dea still hadn't responded. Guido left another message, but no results. After showering and getting dressed, he grabbed a quick bite and left for his office at the stadium to do a follow-up after the game.

As the day wore on he called her several times. No phone calls from Dea proved something was wrong.

After telling Sergio he was leaving, he drove straight to her work only to discover she'd already left for home. By now he was feeling close to frantic. He parked and entered her apartment foyer to ring her. If he couldn't reach her, he would call her parents.

Relief swamped him when he heard the buzz that let him inside. He took the stairs two at a time to the third floor. She'd left the door open for him, but instead of running into his arms, she stood in the living room dressed in her workout clothes. He moved inside and shut the door, struggling for the right words.

"What's going on, Dea?" he rasped. "Why in heaven's name haven't you returned my calls?"

"First let me say welcome back and congratulations on another win."

He rubbed the back of his neck, completely bewildered. "What's happened to you since we kissed goodbye at the airport?"

"If you'll sit down, I'll tell you."

"I'd rather stand."

"Guido, I haven't intentionally tried to be cruel by not answering the phone." Her sincerity smote him. "The truth is, I've needed this much time to gather my thoughts before we spoke again. I had to be sure that you'll understand perfectly what I'm about to tell you."

He felt like he'd been slugged in the gut. "You've decided you don't want to marry me after all."

Her unmistakable nod caused such excruciating pain he couldn't breathe. While he stood there in shock, she walked over to the end table and put the ring down.

"More than anything in the world, I want to marry you and be your wife. But I don't want my husband to give up the career he loves for me."

Her first salvo found its target, crippling him.

"I want the Guido I met, who was full of life and excitement, who's still young and has an extraordinary gift that can't be bought. That man has the ability to motivate thousands of younger men who need a hero to model themselves after. A man like that only comes along once in several lifetimes.

"I fell in love with that man, not the man who's going back to a job he'll still be able to do years from now, a job that doesn't fulfill him, a job that squeezes the life out of him.

"Guido Rossano? You're worried you'll never live up to your father's expectations if you don't go back to the company. *I'm* worried you'll never be happy again if you do, so we need our engagement to end."

Zing. Another salvo to finish him off. He broke out in a cold sweat.

She moved to the doorway. "You're welcome to stay here as long as you want. I'm off to the gym."

In the next instant she was gone, leaving her words ringing in his ears. *I don't want my husband to give up the career he loves for me.*

Little did Dea know he'd already come to his senses and she'd been preaching to the converted. But she hadn't given him the chance to talk.

Galvanized into action, he raced out the door to

stop her. But when he reached her parking space, he discovered her car was still there. She had to have taken the staircase to escape him. Where in the hell was the gym? But even if he could find her, the gym wasn't the place to continue their conversation.

Guido went back to her apartment. After locking the door, he pocketed the ring. A quick examination of the kitchen revealed she had enough food for him to make them a meal. But she didn't come home and he ended up putting the food away.

He sat on the couch to watch the evening news and the sports. At five after eleven he heard her key in the lock and she opened the door. Her eyes collided with his across the expanse. She looked drawn and pale. Her hair had been tied at her nape with a band. "Guido! What are you doing here?"

"What do you think? You disappeared on me before I had a chance to talk to you about anything."

She closed the door. "I can smell garlic and basil."

"I made us a meal. If you're hungry, I'll warm it up."

"I ate dinner earlier."

"By yourself?"

"No. With Gina. We met at the gym first."

He'd been lounging back on the couch with his legs extended. "You told me I could stay as long as I wanted, so I took you at your word. If you're too tired to hear what I have to say right now, I'll still be here in the morning."

Her features wooden, she came closer and sank down on one of the chairs.

"Go ahead."

Guido sat forward. "After I flew to Naples to surprise my family, I discovered they were away for the day with friends in Salerno. I was the one surprised and ended up visiting with my grandfather and his nurse. He mostly talked about the war years and his hard life when he was young."

Her head lifted. "You didn't talk business?"

"No. He told me he always wanted to go to sea and travel the world. But he revered his strict father too much and stuck with the shipping company like a dutiful son. He looked me in the eyes and said, 'My life was successful. I had a loving wife and family, but my great regret was that I wasn't happy in my career. Good for you for doing what makes you happy.' With those words he said he was tired and told me to kiss him before he went to bed."

She rubbed her hands over her knees. "That must have been a very emotional experience for you."

"I heard a side of my grandfather I didn't know existed. Yesterday in Siena I underwent another shock when my parents showed up to be with me at the game."

She looked startled. "They actually came?"

"Yes. I knew it was my grandfather's doing, but the fact that they made the effort was a revelation. My mother had always been on my side and would have come to all my games if she hadn't felt it was disloyal to my father. It was an added bonus for them to see that my team won the game."

"I heard the score on the news," she murmured.

"When I saw them off at the airport and thanked them for coming, I told them I loved owning the team. So much in fact that I wasn't planning to go back to the company for a few years. But to sweeten the bad news, I told them you and I were getting married and wanted him and Mamma to help us plan everything."

Dea's eyes went suspiciously bright.

"I thanked him for never giving up on me and finding me the love of my life."

"You did?" She sounded incredulous.

"Do you know he wept? So did my mother, but I've never seen my father break down like that. Before he had a chance to say another word, I promised him that God willing, we'd give them grandchildren. I also invited them to fly to Ischia with us soon so they can see where we're going to live. We'll let them choose the room they'd like to have when they stay with us."

"Oh, Guido—" Suddenly Dea had launched herself into his arms and broke down sobbing. "Forgive me for the things I said to you, darling. You have to forgive me for doubting you."

He crushed her against him, burying his face in her hair. "I can understand why you said what you did. To be honest, when I was talking to you on the sailboat, I was thinking of my own father, not yours."

"I know that now." She half sobbed the words.

"I've always been afraid he didn't think soccer was a worthy job for a son of his."

"I understand it all. I get it, but you have to know he doesn't feel that way."

"You're right."

She covered his face with kisses. "I never meant to hurt you. Where's my ring?"

"Right here." He reached in his trouser pocket and put it on her finger.

"I swear I'll never take it off again."

Their mouths met hungrily. When he finally lifted his head, he said, "Do you think it's too late to call your parents and tell them our news?"

"Yes, but they'd never forgive me if I didn't waken them anyway. And then I want to phone Alessandra and Rini. She loves you and has wanted this marriage since the day we went out on the cruiser together."

"You made that up."

"No. What you don't know is that she and I have had several talks about you, all my doing. Rini's going to be so happy for us too. Now the *four* of us will be joined at the hip forever."

Guido burst into laughter. Heavens, how he loved this woman! What was it Rini had said that evening at the castle when he'd confided in him about Dea?

You and I both know that no matter how bad it looks, you never leave the stadium until the game is over. Astounding surprises happen in the last second.

Astounding was right. At the last second all Guido's dreams had come true. He stretched out on the couch and started to pull her on top of him, but she held back. "If we don't make the call now, it'll be too late."

"You're right."

She went over by the chair to get her purse and pulled out her phone. He sat up and she rejoined him on the couch. Guido wrapped his arm around her and held her close while she punched the programmed number. "I've got it on speakerphone."

"Dea?" her mother cried after picking up on the third ring. "What's wrong, *tesoro*?"

"Not a thing, Mamma. Can you put your phone on speaker so Papà can hear this too?"

"Just a minute. Okay. Go ahead. We're both listening."

Guido squeezed her hip.

"Do you remember the day you told me to concentrate on finding myself? If I did that, my prince would find me?"

"Prince?" he whispered in her ear.

"Of course I do."

"Well, you're full of wisdom. My blond pirate prince has asked me to marry him."

Pirate?

"Grazie a Dio!" her father said in a booming voice.

"Oh—*tesoro*, we've been praying for this day since your sister's wedding."

She stared at Guido. "You have?"

"We weren't the only ones, either."

"What do you mean?"

"When you and Guido stood at the front of the cathedral as maid of honor and best man, Guido's parents smiled at your father and me. We were all thinking the same thing—that our beautiful son and daughter were meant to be together, but you didn't know it then. I'm so happy for you. Guido? Are you there? Do your parents know yet?"

Dea handed him the phone.

"They know, and they think I'm the luckiest man alive, which I am."

"Welcome to the family, Guido." This from Dea's father.

He felt a thickening in his throat. "I'm thrilled to become a part of it. I don't know if Dea told you, but my father arranged for that fashion show on the yacht so I could meet the breathtaking Dea Loti. He thought she would make me the perfect wife. I took one look at her and knew she would."

"That's very touching," Dea's mother said in a tear-filled voice.

"Mamma? How would you and Papà feel about our getting married in the Rossanos' church in Naples?"

"We don't care where you take your vows as long as we're there," her father asserted.

"Darling? Have you picked a date?"

Dea kissed Guido's lips. "Maybe three weeks? A month? By then I will have graduated and the soccer season will be over. We don't want to wait any longer than that."

"Does Alessandra know?"

"We're going to phone them right now."

"You do that and we'll talk more tomorrow. Fulvia will be overjoyed."

"She will! I guess I don't have to tell you that I have the best parents on earth. *Dormi bene.*"

"Ooh!" Dea threw her arms around him, almost knocking him over. "I'm so happy I can't breathe."

"You have to breathe to live, *adorata*. Come on.

Let's get this call to your sister over with. You and I have things to do."

She kissed one corner of his mouth. "Are you going to make us wait a whole month?"

"Yes, you gorgeous witch. Keeping the fires burning will add infinite pleasure to our wedding night and all the nights destiny allows us from then on."

Dea grasped his hands and kissed the tips of his fingers. "So—" she rolled her eyes at him "—you chip, drop, kick, sweep, cook and are an incredible romantic too. What did I ever do to deserve you?"

June 30, fourteenth-century church of San Giovanni, Carbonara, Naples

"There are so many photographers here you'll be late for your own wedding."

Dea clung to her father's arm, trembling with excitement as she carried a sheaf of white roses tied with a white satin ribbon. "I love you, Papà."

His eyes glazed over with love. "You know how I feel about my daughter."

She did. "I don't know what I'd do without you." People had thronged from everywhere to watch, but all she could think about was Guido, who stood inside the church waiting for her. She couldn't get to him fast enough.

"Juliana outdid herself when she designed your wedding dress. Her gift to you is almost as magnificent as you are, my darling girl."

The exquisite lace covering her arms and shoulders

hugged her white princess-style wedding dress. She wore a shoulder-length veil of the same lace and had left her hair long. Guido asked that she never cut it. Since he felt that strongly, she wanted to please him.

Organ music filled the vestibule where Alessandra and Rini were waiting for them dressed in their wedding finery. Her twin's smiling gaze fused with Dea's. They heard the chords of the wedding march at the same time. This wasn't like the pretend weddings they'd staged in their play castle when they were little. This was really going to happen.

Two friends of the Rossano family opened the doors and Dea began the long walk to the front of the church with her handsome father. Alessandra and Rini followed them down the aisle. The church overflowed with guests from both their families. With every step closer to Guido and the priest who would marry them, her heart thudded harder and harder.

Out of the corner of her eye she saw some friends from the college and the models she'd worked with over the years. With another step, she spotted Gina and Aldo and realized everyone from Juliana's shop, including her staff, had come.

Farther on, she saw Sergio and the other men and coaches who worked with Guido. Many of the players on his team had come to honor him. Still others from Rossano Shipping Lines had come en masse.

Closer to the altar she saw the Montanari family, including Valentina and Giovanni, Rini's sister- and brother-in-law. They sat on one side of the aisle. On the other sat her loving mother and aunt Fulvia, plus the staff from the castle. Juliana and her husband sat behind them. The older woman beamed. Dea owed her so much.

Suddenly her father walked her to Guido's side and lifted the roses to hand to her sister. Dea turned toward her fiancé, but she couldn't prevent the slight gasp of awe that escaped her lips.

With his tall superb physique and dark blond hair, he looked so splendid she almost fainted. A white rose decorated the lapel of his wedding suit, the same midnight blue color as his eyes. Guido wore his jacket buttoned over a matching vest with a stark white shirt and pastel gray-blue tie. He flashed her a haunting smile that took her breath away.

"Bellissima," he whispered in a husky tone and grasped her hand. *"Grazie a Dio* you're no longer a figment of my imagination. If you had any idea how long I've been waiting for this moment…"

She *did*, actually, because she'd been in the same pain.

As the ceremony began, she feared the Rossanos' family priest performing the rites could hear her heart resounding throughout the nave. Very little registered until they'd repeated their vows to love and honor each other.

"I now pronounce you man and wife and ask that you remain faithful to each other. May God bless this union. In the name of the Father and the Son." He made the sign of the cross. "Amen."

Guido didn't wait for any prompting. He reached for her shoulders and lowered his mouth to hers, giv-

ing her what she would always remember…the divine
kiss of life from her new husband. Unspeakable joy
filled her heart.

For three days and nights they stayed in their suite
at the villa on Ischia, the only area aside from the
bathroom that had been furnished in time for their
honeymoon.

This morning Guido had left her arms long enough
to go down to the village for more food. So far they'd
subsisted on love and little else.

Dea's hungry eyes played over his hard-muscled
body as he put some sacks on the table. He was the
most gorgeous man on earth, whether in shorts and a
T-shirt like he was wearing, or nothing at all.

"I brought you something that will interest you."

"I thought by now you'd figured out that you are
my only interest."

A smile of satisfaction lit up his handsome face. He
drew a newspaper out of one of the bags and handed
it to her. "Look on page two. No doubt my father had
a great deal to do with the half-page article and picture in the *Corriere della Sera.*"

She smiled up at him. "The paper with the larg-
est circulation in Italy? Of course he did. He's the
proud *papà.*"

Dea propped herself against the pillows. The second she opened to the article, she let out a cry. There
she was in her flowing white wedding gown and veil
coming out of the church with Guido in a formal dark

suit hugging her waist. The happiness on their faces brought tears to her eyes as she read the article.

On June 30, Signor and Signora Guido Ernesto Fortunati Rossano were married in the fourteenth-century church of San Giovanni a Carbonara in Naples. A reception followed at the Rossano villa. The island of Ischia will be home to the famous couple.

The bride, gorgeous former supermodel now turned opera-wardrobe designer Dea Caracciolo, is the twenty-eight-year-old daughter of Count Onorato Caracciolo and Princess Taranto of Southern Italy.

The groom, thirty-two-year-old Guido, the son of prominent shipping magnate Leonides Rossano and Isabella Fortunati, and the grandson of Ernesto Rossano, is the former national soccer champion of Italy known as the *Cuor di Leone*. At present he is the new owner of the fast-rising soccer team Scatto Roma. The team is tied for first place with Team Venezia, and the two will compete in a play-off for the national championship July 3 at the Emanuele Soccer Stadium in Rome.

Dea put down the newspaper. "I think the reporter got it all in and then some."

"Do you mind? You know Papà."

"Darling, I love him. He's your father and I love

his son so terribly that if you don't get in bed and love me this instant, I won't survive another minute."

"Well, we can't have that." He removed his clothes with startling speed and slid beneath the quilt to roll her on her back. "Dea," he whispered, looking down at her. "I keep thinking we're in a dream and I'm going to wake up. We aren't dreaming, are we?"

"I don't think so, and I'm afraid you're stuck with a wanton for good."

"If every man were stuck with a passionate woman like you, we'd all be in permanent heaven."

"Honestly? H-has it been good for you?" Her voice faltered.

He shook his dark blond head. "Can't you tell what you do to me? For three days I haven't let you leave my arms. You're so beautiful, I'm constantly out of breath. If you could see the way you look with your hair spread out on the pillow, and the way your eyes darken with emotion, maybe you'd understand. But you're not a man."

"Thank heaven for that. You make me thankful I'm a woman." Her eyes filled with tears. "I wish we'd met ten years ago. When I think of the time we've wasted."

"I try not to think about it. What matters is now. You've made me happier than I could ever have imagined. Love me again, *squisita*." He lowered his mouth to hers and began to make love to her with a new ferocity. For the next few hours Dea was shaken by a passion she'd never known.

Her amazing husband had been so wise to insist

they wait until they were married to become intimate lovers. To experience the wonder of lovemaking like this without knowing you belonged to each other first would take away this ultimate joy.

They finally fell asleep again. Later he wakened her with a hungry kiss. "How would you like to sleep on the boat tonight? I thought it was time we christened that bedroom too."

She chuckled. "I agree. Why don't we eat and then go sailing?"

"Are you saying that for my sake?"

Dea gave him an impish grin. "Yes! Because I can tell you're suddenly restless. The game on Sunday is on your mind. I'm thinking about it too. Tomorrow we'll be flying back to Rome. Before we leave, I want to spend our last night on the *Bona Dea*. She *is* the goddess of fertility."

His blue eyes flickered with emotion. "Would you really like to start a family right away?"

"Yes, if we can. But if you don't feel that way…"

He kissed her deeply. "I want it all with you as fast as possible."

"I'm so glad you said that. We're not getting any younger. It would be so nice if we had a baby soon who would become friends with Brazzo. They're planning on adopting another baby one of these days."

"I know. Rini told me."

"When did he tell you that?"

"Yesterday evening while you were in the shower, he left me a message that they were negotiating for another baby. According to Alessandra, it will be the closest thing to having twins. He said he hoped I was doing my own form of negotiation in order to get the job done too. He ended with, 'Hurry.'"

She sat straight up. "He didn't!"

"Oh, yes, he did. Do you want to see my phone?"

"No. You two are incorrigible. Alessandra would have a cow if she knew he'd written that to you."

"A cow?"

"It's an American expression Gina picked up from Aldo's New York friend and she passed it on to me."

He grabbed her hand and pressed it against his heart. "I swear I'll keep it a secret from my new sister-in-law." In the next breath he threw off the quilt. She screamed, provoking his laughter.

"Come on, Aphrodite. Even your lover, who can never get enough of you, has to renew his energy, and I'm starving!"

October 10, Posso Island, Southern Italy

The sun had just fallen into the water. "There they are!" Dea had glimpsed the Jeep behind the castle as the helicopter dipped closer. "This is so exciting to be having a reunion here at last!"

Once they landed, Guido hugged her hips before helping her down. Every time he touched her, her legs turned to jelly. She hurried toward the Jeep and saw that her sister had brought Brazzo with them. He was seated on her lap playing with his purple octopus, tugging on one of the belled tentacles.

Their dark-haired fourteen-month-old toddler was

so adorable Dea could hardly stand it. With coloring like that and olive skin, you'd never know he wasn't their birth son.

"Oh, you cute little thing." She kissed his cheeks and then her sister's cheek before climbing in the back.

"What? No kiss for me?" Rini teased.

"How about a hug instead?" She wrapped her arm around his neck from behind. Guido followed her into the backseat with their luggage.

"It's about time you lovebirds left the nest." This from Rini. Dea saw the secret look the two men flashed each other.

"We've been busy decorating the house," Guido explained.

"Sure you have. Excuses, excuses." Rini kept up the banter.

Alessandra laughed. "I hope you're hungry. Dinner is waiting."

Dea reached forward to tousle Brazzo's curls. "I'm starving. Someone should have warned me that getting married makes you hungry. Are Mamma and Papà here?"

"They will be later." Alessandra looked over her shoulder at Guido. "How does the team look to you for this new season?"

"It's good. They've recovered from the loss in July and are working harder than ever. Dante's back with us and suiting up. Another month and the doctor will clear him to play."

"That's wonderful news."

Rini drove them around to the entrance of the castle. Dea got out behind Alessandra and trailed her
into the foyer, where Alfredo was waiting. "Oh, my
buddy." She scooped him up. "Have you missed me?"

But at this point Brazzo was toddling around and
the cat squirmed to get down. "Well, I just got my
question answered. This fickle cat has a new play-
mate. Look at you walking, Brazzo!"

The men had just come inside with the bags. They
all watched in amusement as the precious boy chased
after the housekeeper's pet.

"Come on, you two." Rini started for the stairs.
"We've put you in the same bedroom Guido has used
when he's stayed here."

"Brazzo and I will be in the dining room, won't
we, sweetheart. Hurry back down."

Dea hugged her sister, then followed the men upstairs. Excitement rippled through her body to think
she'd be sleeping with Guido in her old home.

Rini left them alone while they freshened up. Guido
grabbed her from behind while she was looking out
the window. "You have no idea how I longed to drag
you up here after our soccer match on the sand. The
dreams I had about you would make your face turn
crimson."

She wheeled around and threw her arms around his
neck. "I had my own dreams that night. The thought
of sneaking into your bedroom in the middle of the
night never left my mind. I guess I don't have to wonder what you would have done. You would have been

the total gentleman and escorted me back to the hall-way."

"Don't be so sure. I was on fire for you that night."

"So on fire you didn't even say goodbye to me."

"You know why, my love. Come on. We'll have all night to finish this conversation. In the meantime, our hosts are waiting."

They clasped hands and went downstairs to the dining room. Brazzo was sitting in his high chair at the corner of the table between Rini and Alessandra. He banged the tray with a spoon.

Dea chuckled and sat across from them with Guido. "Umm. I can see the cook has outdone herself with my favorite salmon and eggplant."

"She knew you were coming and remembered."

"I'll go out to the kitchen later and thank her."

"Now that we're all here, Rini and I have an announcement." Dea eyed Guido while they waited for Alessandra's news. "We had to be certain to make sure everything was going right, but we have just been told to expect our next baby in a month!"

"I knew it!" Dea squealed in delight.

"It's a girl this time." Rini's smile lit up his dark eyes.

"There couldn't be better news, *paisano*," Guido said.

"I agree, but do you think you can stand a little more?" Dea reached in the pocket of her pleated pants for a picture. "We've got a little news of our own."

The shocked look on Guido's face was worth all

the trouble she'd taken to keep her secret to herself. "Dea?" he whispered huskily.

"It's Rini's fault."

Everyone looked shocked at her comment, especially her brother-in-law. "You did send my husband a text four months ago. I'll quote it for everyone.

"'We're negotiating for another baby. According to Alessandra, it will be the closest thing to having twins. I hope you're doing your own form of negotiation in order to get the job done too.' Your postscript said, 'Hurry.'"

While quiet reigned, she handed Guido the picture. "Take a look and see what you did, darling."

Her husband looked down at the sonogram like he was in a trance.

"If you'll notice, there are two babies in there."

"Dea!" Alessandra's cry of joy reverberated in the dining room and probably the whole castle. She shot out of her chair and hurried around to look at it over Guido's shoulder.

"There *are* two."

"One is a girl. The doctor couldn't tell the gender of the other one yet. I'm four months along."

"Then our daughters will be less than six months apart. That's so perfect! We'll get out the play castle when they're old enough."

"It'll be déjà vu."

"Wait till our parents hear about this—"

Guido was still processing the information in a daze. He turned to Dea. "I thought you'd been putting on weight recently, but I didn't want to say anything."

"I knew you had to have noticed." She leaned over and kissed him on the mouth. "Sorry if I worried you about that."

"I wasn't worried, Dea."

"Liar. I love you more than ever for not giving me grief about it."

He got to his feet. "Are you all right?" When he put his hands on her upper arms, he was trembling. "Is everything going the way it should?"

"The doctor has given me a clean bill of health."

Alessandra ran the picture around to show Rini. While everyone was occupied, their parents walked in. "What's going on?" their father wanted to know.

Dea smiled at him. "We all have news, Papà. You go first, Alessandra."

Once her sister told them that they would be getting a girl within the month, she ran back around to give Dea the picture. "Now it's your turn."

The moment was surreal as she handed her mother the sonogram. She watched her parents study it.

Suddenly her mother pressed a hand over her heart. "Twins… You're going to have twins."

Her dad smiled broadly. "Well, what do you know. Fulvia said twins ran in the Taranto side of the family. Thanks to the Montanari side of the family, we're going to have a set of twins before another set comes along."

Dea loved her father intensely for making Rini feel included in a very real way.

"Let's break out the champagne, but you won't be able to drink it, Dea. No alcohol until after the babies are born," her father informed her. "Your mother and I know every rule."

Dea lifted shining eyes to Alessandra. "But you, my dear sister, can have all you want."

Rini hugged her. "I'm afraid it's wasted on my wife."

"Dea?" Guido whispered in her ear. "I need to be alone with you. Can we go upstairs soon?"

She nodded and kissed his jaw. He'd just found out he was going to be the father of twins. That had to be staggering news for any man. Perhaps even as staggering as it had been for the woman who carried them.

Her mother seemed to understand what was going on. "Dea, honey, you look tired. I think you should go up to bed. We'll celebrate in the morning."

Bless you, Mamma.

"Bed does sound good. It's been a long day."

Now that the evening had come to an end, everyone said good-night. Guido put his arm around her waist as they climbed the stairs to the bedroom on the third floor. "Oh, I forgot the picture."

"We'll get it in the morning. Right now I want to take care of you."

She hadn't realized that having to keep her news a secret from Guido had drained her. Suddenly she felt relaxed and couldn't wait to drift off with his arms around her.

As soon as she brushed her teeth and undressed,

she fell into bed. "I know you want your parents to know. Why don't you give them a call? Then I'll answer every question. I'm sorry I didn't tell you before now, but when the doctor detected two heartbeats, I wanted to wait until he could take a picture and make sure the babies were healthy. I couldn't see worrying you until I had to."

"I'm not upset with you, Dea. If anything, I'm glad I didn't know before now. We've had to deal with the villa and work, your graduation. But now that I know, I'm going to make certain you take perfect care of yourself. We have two precious babies growing inside you. It's a thrill I still haven't fully comprehended yet."

"That's the way I felt when the doctor first told me. Go on and phone your parents. They'll be ecstatic."

He put the covers over her and sat on the edge of the bed to call his family. The joy in their voices rang out through the phone. Dea reached for it. "We don't know if there's a boy or another girl in there. Maybe by the next appointment the doctor will be able to tell us."

"You're going to need help," his mother said through the tears.

"We'll need a lot of it," Dea assured her and meant it. "I'm so thankful we already have your room ready at the villa. Here's Guido back."

She waited while he finished talking to his parents. By the time he'd hung up and gotten into bed, she was half gone.

"You know that song...he had the whole world in his arms... Those words were written for me."

Dea turned into him, loving his hard, solid strength. "It works both ways. She had the whole world in her arms... You're my whole world, Guido Rossano.

"My whole glorious world. *Ti amo.*"

* * * * *

MILLS & BOON®
Hardback – November 2016

ROMANCE

Di Sione's Virgin Mistress	Sharon Kendrick
Snowbound with His Innocent Temptation	Cathy Williams
The Italian's Christmas Child	Lynne Graham
A Diamond for Del Rio's Housekeeper	Susan Stephens
Claiming His Christmas Consequence	Michelle Smart
One Night with Gael	Maya Blake
Married for the Italian's Heir	Rachael Thomas
Unwrapping His Convenient Fiancée	Melanie Milburne
Christmas Baby for the Princess	Barbara Wallace
Greek Tycoon's Mistletoe Proposal	Kandy Shepherd
The Billionaire's Prize	Rebecca Winters
The Earl's Snow-Kissed Proposal	Nina Milne
The Nurse's Christmas Gift	Tina Beckett
The Midwife's Pregnancy Miracle	Kate Hardy
Their First Family Christmas	Alison Roberts
The Nightshift Before Christmas	Annie O'Neil
It Started at Christmas...	Janice Lynn
Unwrapped by the Duke	Amy Ruttan
Hold Me, Cowboy	Maisey Yates
Holiday Baby Scandal	Jules Bennett

MILLS & BOON®
Large Print – November 2016

ROMANCE

Di Sione's Innocent Conquest	Carol Marinelli
A Virgin for Vasquez	Cathy Williams
The Billionaire's Ruthless Affair	Miranda Lee
Master of Her Innocence	Chantelle Shaw
Moretti's Marriage Command	Kate Hewitt
The Flaw in Raffaele's Revenge	Annie West
Bought by Her Italian Boss	Dani Collins
Wedded for His Royal Duty	Susan Meier
His Cinderella Heiress	Marion Lennox
The Bridesmaid's Baby Bump	Kandy Shepherd
Bound by the Unborn Baby	Bella Bucannon

HISTORICAL

The Unexpected Marriage of Gabriel Stone	Louise Allen
The Outcast's Redemption	Sarah Mallory
Claiming the Chaperon's Heart	Anne Herries
Commanded by the French Duke	Meriel Fuller
Unbuttoning the Innocent Miss	Bronwyn Scott

MEDICAL

Tempted by Hollywood's Top Doc	Louisa George
Perfect Rivals...	Amy Ruttan
English Rose in the Outback	Lucy Clark
A Family for Chloe	Lucy Clark
The Doctor's Baby Secret	Scarlet Wilson
Married for the Boss's Baby	Susan Carlisle

MILLS & BOON®
Hardback – December 2016

ROMANCE

A Di Sione for the Greek's Pleasure	Kate Hewitt
The Prince's Pregnant Mistress	Maisey Yates
The Greek's Christmas Bride	Lynne Graham
The Guardian's Virgin Ward	Caitlin Crews
A Royal Vow of Convenience	Sharon Kendrick
The Desert King's Secret Heir	Annie West
Married for the Sheikh's Duty	Tara Pammi
Surrendering to the Vengeful Italian	Angela Bissell
Winter Wedding for the Prince	Barbara Wallace
Christmas in the Boss's Castle	Scarlet Wilson
Her Festive Doorstep Baby	Kate Hardy
Holiday with the Mystery Italian	Ellie Darkins
White Christmas for the Single Mum	Susanne Hampton
A Royal Baby for Christmas	Scarlet Wilson
Playboy on Her Christmas List	Carol Marinelli
The Army Doc's Baby Bombshell	Sue MacKay
The Doctor's Sleigh Bell Proposal	Susan Carlisle
The Baby Proposal	Andrea Laurence
Maid Under the Mistletoe	Maureen Child

MILLS & BOON®
Large Print – December 2016

ROMANCE

The Di Sione Secret Baby	Maya Blake
Carides's Forgotten Wife	Maisey Yates
The Playboy's Ruthless Pursuit	Miranda Lee
His Mistress for a Week	Melanie Milburne
Crowned for the Prince's Heir	Sharon Kendrick
In the Sheikh's Service	Susan Stephens
Marrying Her Royal Enemy	Jennifer Hayward
An Unlikely Bride for the Billionaire	Michelle Douglas
Falling for the Secret Millionaire	Kate Hardy
The Forbidden Prince	Alison Roberts
The Best Man's Guarded Heart	Katrina Cudmore

HISTORICAL

Sheikh's Mail-Order Bride	Marguerite Kaye
Miss Marianne's Disgrace	Georgie Lee
Her Enemy at the Altar	Virginia Heath
Enslaved by the Desert Trader	Greta Gilbert
Royalist on the Run	Helen Dickson

MEDICAL

The Prince and the Midwife	Robin Gianna
His Pregnant Sleeping Beauty	Lynne Marshall
One Night, Twin Consequences	Annie O'Neil
Twin Surprise for the Single Doc	Susanne Hampton
The Doctor's Forbidden Fling	Karin Baine
The Army Doc's Secret Wife	Charlotte Hawkes

MILLS & BOON®

Why shop at millsandboon.co.uk?

Each year, thousands of romance readers find their perfect read at millsandboon.co.uk. That's because we're passionate about bringing you the very best romantic fiction. Here are some of the advantages of shopping at www.millsandboon.co.uk:

* **Get new books first**—you'll be able to buy your favourite books one month before they hit the shops

* **Get exclusive discounts**—you'll also be able to buy our specially created monthly collections, with up to 50% off the RRP

* **Find your favourite authors**—latest news, interviews and new releases for all your favourite authors and series on our website, plus ideas for what to try next

* **Join in**—once you've bought your favourite books, don't forget to register with us to rate, review and join in the discussions

Visit **www.millsandboon.co.uk**
for all this and more today!